the Lily of Life

The Lily of Life

The Lily Of Life

Copyright © 2014 Lire Classics

By The Crown Princess Of Roumania
With a preface by Carmen Sylva;
Illustrations by Helen Stratton.

Printed originally by Hazell, Watson & Viney, Ld., London and Aylesbury, c1913.

ISBN-10: 1939652723
ISBN-13: 978-1-939652-72-0

Lire Classics is an imprint of Lire Books LLC.

Book Website
www.LireBooks.com
Email: contact@LireBooks.com

Give feedback on the book at:
feedback@LireBooks.com

Printed in U.S.A

Dedicated

To My Daughter
Elisabetha

"because we love the same beauties
and understand the same dreams"

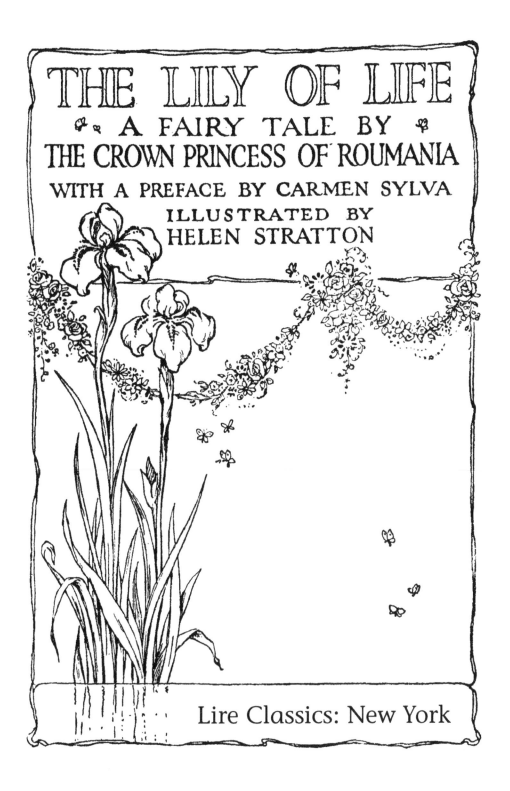

THE LILY OF LIFE

A FAIRY TALE BY
THE CROWN PRINCESS OF ROUMANIA

WITH A PREFACE BY CARMEN SYLVA
ILLUSTRATED BY
HELEN STRATTON

Lire Classics: New York

Illustrations

Page

Preface

A YOUNG mother, who is a true artist, relating a fairy tale, is one of the greatest joys in this world.

The first impression of this most delightful story is the feeling for colour and decoration, then the love of flowers and nature in general, and then enough experience to show Life's tragic side as in a looking-glass that is very pure and bright. The story becomes more and more touching, the Sacuntala or Psyche it represents more and more interesting and lovable.

The great incentive to every sacrifice, Love, is represented in all its strength and purity. The whole book will be a true enjoyment to young and old, the one looking for the sequel of the story, the other taken up by the philosophy and inner meaning. There has been more than one Damaianti in this world, more than one woman's feet have bled on their road to eternity, more than one woman has had to sacrifice everything, her heart and soul, and youth and beauty, the very hair of her head. More than one woman has remained without a reward, and has gone down to history as a martyr and a saint. Here is one more.

Her sufferings are so real, her sacrifice is so complete – woman's lot in all its tragic reality.

We read it with deep emotion, and our feelings are the stronger, as great beauty pervades it all, and every situation is so entirely picturesque. All readers of fairy lore will find it true and beautiful. Fairyland is our last refuge, when the world is a battle-field and religion gone. Then fairyland steps in, and everything becomes alive again – love and piety and beauty and ideals. God has blessed fairyland and given it to the little ones, to keep their dear hearts pure and bright. Every mother ought to be inspired by the lovely eyes that look into hers with such utter confidence and with such great expectations.

CARMEN SYLVA.

Lily of Life

In a beautiful castle by the sea, a castle all of golden tiles, so worked that it looked as if it were made of solid, beaten gold – a gold which had taken the wonderful tint of autumn leaves – there lived a king and queen – a happy king and queen. Happy, because their reign had been successful, and they were loved by their people, and had seen what they had undertaken flourish and become a happiness to those they ruled, so that it all fell back in blessings upon themselves. They were happy, too, because they had always loved each other, and because they had beautiful twin daughters. Certainly, sometimes when it was raining outside, or when they heard sad news, so that all seemed a little less bright than usual, they would regret they had no son; but, as I tell you, this king and queen only thought of it on rainy days, when the sun did not manage, in spite of its force, to pierce the clouds. But that was seldom, because their land was a bright one, where flowers grew in abundance, and people smiled more often than they cried. And then their two daughters were – oh, so beautiful! Exactly alike, except that one had golden hair, with great, dreamy, rather sad brown eyes, and the other had jet black hair, with a blue shine in the light, and her eyes as well were blue – great bright blue eyes, fringed with feathery black lashes. This one was called Mora; she had a sweet voice and a happy laugh. Her golden-haired sister was called Corona, because, when she was born, her hair was so bright that it seemed as if she had a crown on her head. But her old nurse had shaken her head when she looked into her deep, sad, brown eyes, and had wondered why already, at that early age, she should have that strange look of painful knowledge. She had said: "In spite of that golden crown on her head, it seems to me as if she carried the sadness of the world within her"; but the others laughed, and they seemed to be right, because Corona grew up as bright and happy as her beautiful sister. They were inseparable friends, and nothing was more enchanting than to see those two beautiful creatures coming hand in hand up the steps of the great marble terraces that led down to the sea; both so indescribably beautiful, and as if made out of the same mould, so wonderfully alike were they; the same height, the same build, the same features, the same slim, tall figures, the only difference being in their hair and eyes. Both had voices of such extreme sweetness, that when they sat on the seashore together, singing, the seagulls would stop in their flight to listen, and the impatient little waves, that continually kissed the sand, would try to come nearer so as to hear more easily. The King and Queen loved them with a passionate love, and would sit upon the terrace above, leaning over to watch all their movements with never-ending interest; and the two sisters would turn their sweet faces up towards them, and in their eyes one could see that they were grateful for the love of their parents.

The castle was like a fairy castle, high up, overlooking the sea, and terrace upon terrace of green marble led down to the silver-sanded shore. There was a long flight of golden steps on each side, guarded by a line of tall cypresses; and when you looked up along it it seemed like Jacob's ladder. But only those who felt very nimble cared to climb it daily; others shook their heads and smiled, but preferred to think of Jacob's angels flying upwards, using their snow white wings, which is, it seems, not at all a tiring way of climbing stairs.

The twin Princesses were as happy as the day was long, and although they were already sixteen, they still had many studies. A very old philosopher, with a long grey beard, wrapped in a dark-blue, golden-bordered robe, came every day with a very big book, and they would sit under a huge spreading tree, covered with a wealth of orange-red flowers. The book would be laid on a large white marble table inlaid with golden mosaic, which was cool to the touch; and with their young faces brought close to the old one, they would eagerly lean over the huge volume, ready to learn all the wisdom the old philosopher could teach them. But some things he did not know, so some of their questions remained un answered. For instance, he could not tell them what colours God used to paint the butterflies, nor why Mora had black hair, whilst her sister's was golden; nor could he tell them for certain what Heaven was like, and if they would meet there all the stern figures of their ancestors, looking like the beautiful pictures in the big castle gallery; nor was he sure what the wind told, nor what the sea complained of, nor what the seagulls were always screaming out to each other. And yet the Princesses wanted badly to know these things, and sometimes the merry eyed Mora would say: "Old man! old man! We love you very much, and we are impressed by your knowledge, but we do think you are not quite, quite as learned as we hoped!" Then both would laugh, and the old man would lift his head, smile at them, and love their youth and the sweetness of spring that was about them.

The Twin Princesses

Both sisters loved the sea, and they had a golden boat shaped like an eagle, with a sail of violet silk, upon which a golden sword with a hilt like a cross was woven. The golden sword, passed through a circlet of silver, was the emblem of their family, and meant that their arms were always used for what was holy and right. And when they sailed over the sapphire blue sea, their golden and raven locks mingling in the wind, their sweet voices charming the waves, the old sailors used to sit and smile, and the hearts of the young ones would beat faster; the sun would look down upon the two girls and wonder at their beauty, and the grey and white seagulls would circle round their ship, making patterns with their wings to attract their attention. And in the beautiful evenings, when the sun was sinking, turning the sea into a blazing pool of blood, they would sit side by side as their ship drifted homewards. Corona would work at a beautiful embroidery on silver cloth, representing golden eagles, holding in their claws a bleeding heart; Mora, always more idle, would lean her head against her sister's shoulder and make her laugh with all the tales she told. Or they would sit silent, hand in hand, watching the fire-coloured sky turn into orange and yellow, till night crept slowly over all, wrapping sea and sky in a dark grey shroud. Then they would feel how they loved each other, and they would tighten the grasp of their hands, for fear of any shadow coming between them.

As is usual with parents, the King and Queen, although they adored their children above all in the world, were continually thinking of marrying them; but the two sisters would not hear of it, because they shuddered at the idea of being separated, even for a day.

Around the castle were magnificent forests, and the two Princesses would ride through them together, each followed by her own page. The two pages, Doric and Yno, were young boys, passionately devoted to their mistresses, understanding and feeling their ladies' desires even before they expressed them aloud. Mora and Corona each possessed a horse the colour of her hair; Mora's was inky black, and Corona's was like shining gold; and they would fly along for hours, untiring amidst the glory of the woods. The trees grew strong and straight, their branches joined overhead like the vaulting of a green cathedral, and various flowers grew in different parts, always one kind in each place, but then in such thick masses, that they were like a sea of colour. From afar the blaze of colour could be seen, and then the sisters would loosen the reins, letting their horses fly along till they reached the oasis of colour they had seen from afar shining between the trees; sometimes it seemed like a blue sheet of water; but when they reached the spot it was seen to be millions and millions of blue irises and hyacinths, growing in prodigious masses, and smelling, oh, so sweet! Then, again, in another part the forest would seem as though in flames, which turned out to be a blazing field of orange poppies; and intertwined round the trunks of the trees, growing up in the branches and falling down again in festoons, were orange-coloured roses. In another place it would seem to you that you saw snow in the distance, shining in a sheet of white, but on reaching the spot you would find a carpet of delicate snowdrops. Then, again, it might be a field of yellow cowslips and primroses, or a blaze of tiger-lilies, or a sweet mass of pink carnations the size of roses. It was a blessed country where all those flowers bloomed in the same season.

One day, as the sisters penetrated deep into the forest, they came to a shining pool of dark water, a sort of deep large hole, that looked as if it were bottomless. They were hot from their long gallop, so they slid off their faithful horses, and both stood leaning against them, as the thirsty animals stretched their glossy necks to reach the cool water. There they stood, the dark green forest behind them, and in the distance a gleaming stripe of orange poppies, the golden and black steeds standing quite still, and the beautiful forms of the young girls in their black and gold dresses with wreaths of red roses in their wonderful hair, the whole reflected in the clear dark water beneath. Long they peered into the depth beneath them; then Mora raised her head, and found herself gazing into a pair of large grey eyes on the opposite bank. For a moment it seemed to her like a vision, all had been so still around them, no sound had warned them of another presence. Then she noticed further, that the eyes were set in a beautiful face framed in a golden helmet; and as the green branches parted a wonderful figure of a knight stood before them. Mora seized Corona's hand, and she too became aware of the shining vision; then all three stood spellbound, gazing at each other, speechless, silent with the great emotion clutching at their hearts. Suddenly the knight moved and came forward round the pool, and bending a knee to the ground he bared his head, and his red-brown curls shone like burnished copper. He remained thus in a position of adoration till Mora moved forward, and in a voice trembling with sweet shyness addressed him:

"Noble knight! Kneel not before us, but rise and tell us if there is aught we can do for thee. Hast thou come from far? Hast thou lamed thy steed?"

For a moment he remained silent, overcome by so much sweetness. Then he rose and stood upright before them, long and straight like a golden sun-ray in his glistening armour. At last he spoke:

"Sweet visions of another world! I have indeed come from afar, and I have lost my way in this endless forest, lured onwards by the beauty of all I saw; but now I see it was God's will, so that I should

The Forest Pool

look upon the most perfect of all His works, and I would fain kiss the hem of your robes, in token of homage!"

"Nay," answered Mora again, "tell us thy name, and come with us that we may show the way out of this forest and take thee to our father's castle."

"My name is Ilario; I am the son of the old king of yonder mountainous country. Surely God hath sent me unto you so that my soul should rejoice!" Corona kept her eyes on the youth's face, but answered nothing, and it seemed to her as if a little bird were fluttering beneath her jewelled bodice. Mora called the two pages, who were standing a little distance away, and told one of them to gallop off and tell the King, her father, that they were bringing back a royal guest, and that she and her sister bade him prepare a reception worthy of him. Doric galloped off immediately to fulfil his mistress's bidding, whilst Yno, Corona's page, held the Princesses' horses and helped them to mount. Prince Ilario had left his steed not far off, a glorious dark brown, with white face and four white feet, whose coat was so silky that one could see one's face reflected in its glossy flanks.

They rode on all three together; Corona silent, and Mora's sweet voice rousing echoes amongst the great trees, that bent down their heads to listen. All three felt a strange happiness in their hearts, which had never come to them before. They had reached a long avenue of dark velvety moss, soft as a Persian carpet, and smooth as velvet, and so long that the eye could not reach the end. There they let their steeds gallop side by side, and their hearts seemed full of the sunshine around them. Only Yno, who galloped at a little distance behind them, felt suddenly, as he gazed upon the flying forms before him, as if a cold wind had passed over his soul, and as if his heart was suddenly very lonely. A large eagle, who was soaring far overhead, looked down, and remained poised a few seconds quite motionless above them; he was very old, and had seen much, and flown over many countries, and realized that what he saw now was more beautiful than all he had known before. He felt sad, too, knowing the world with all its burden of sorrow.

Doric's message had been received with joy, and when the sisters arrived with their guest the palace doors stood wide open, and dark blue carpets, with golden crowns woven upon them, had been spread along the marble terraces, blood-red roses had been strewn all the way, and beneath the golden porch stood the King and Queen with their crowns upon their heads, and kind hands outstretched in welcome. The bells were ringing, and from the tower windows sweet music was heard, with lovely voices singing hymns of welcome. Prince Ilario dismounted and bent his knee before his royal hosts, who greeted him with kind words, and led him into the large stone hall, all decorated with the old flags that were the honour and pride of the country. Before an enormous hearth stood a carved table of old oak, laden with golden dishes full of exquisite food, and wonderful fruit in jasper bowls, and dark purple clematis flowers were strewn upon the golden cloth.

That evening there were great rejoicings, and the King had given orders that the sea along the shore should be illuminated with red lights. All the nobles of the country had flocked together, so that merry voices and happy laughter were heard from one green terrace to the other. On the upper one, upon their thrones, sat the King and Queen; but Corona and Mora, with their handsome guest between them, leaned over the rose-entwined balustrade and talked about all that they were eager to impart to each other. And sometimes they were silent, looking at the beautiful, restless sea in the flaming light, but each was ever conscious of the other's presence.

That night both sisters went up to bed, holding each other's hands and singing, because of the lightness of their hearts. It was long before sleep closed their eyes, and when it did come it overtook them with a smile upon their lips. . . .

And now followed days of gaiety, when feast followed feast; and the three young people were inseparable companions, either sailing on the sea, or rambling in the great forest on horseback, or wandering over the beautiful terraces, or in the gardens, and dancing in the great hall at night.

Those were days of wonderful joy, days when the same love began to blossom in the three young hearts, but when no shadow as yet darkened their happiness. Ilario was so handsome to look upon, that no woman's heart remained unmoved at the sight of him.

The two sisters, who had always lived alone with their parents, suddenly discovered a new meaning in life, yet they hardly realized that the strange new gladness was caused by the presence of their wonderful guest.

To do the Prince honour the King proclaimed a great tournament, to be held at his castle. All the noble youths of the country were bidden to try their skill, and on a beautiful summer morning they all rode forth in a gay procession, their steeds decked with trappings of many colours. The sun shone down on the brave company, flashing upon bright swords and lances, and making all the armour blaze in the light. Last of all rode the golden-clad Ilario on his great brown stallion, his head held high, his eyes shining bright with youth and hope, a smile on his lips and a song in his heart. All the spectators knew that no other knight among the company could compare with him. He was braver than them all, stronger than them all; none could keep pace with him, none could overcome him. In the thickest of the melee his golden armour was seen everywhere like a moving sun.

He overthrew all his opponents, with such youthful ardour, yet with such courtly grace, that not even his rivals felt bitter against him, but bowed before his great strength and his kingly charm.

The sisters could not take their eyes off him, and each time he won a new victory their delight was expressed by cries of applause.

When the tournament was over, he rode up to the low balcony from which they leaned down towards him. With shining eyes, and a little breathless, he paid them homage. The sweat streamed from his noble steed, but Ilario sat like a golden statue upon his saddle, showing no signs of fatigue. He doffed his helmet, bowing his head to receive the wreath of roses which the sisters had wound for him. His brown curls lay matted on his brow, and in his eyes, as he gazed up, shone such love, that Corona and Mora felt their hearts leap within them.

From that day each sister carried about with her a secret, one she could not share with the other, the first secret that had ever existed between them.

One day, about three weeks after Ilario's arrival, the page Yno, looking for his mistress, found her beneath a great tree, upon a marble seat, her head hidden against its back, and all around her streamed her golden hair, hiding her face; and it seemed to him that her shoulders were heaving, as if with sobs. Overcome with an intolerable anxiety, which his faithful heart seemed to feel with an unnatural lucidity, he sank upon the ground beside her, and like a faithful dog touched her hand with his lips. Corona turned with a start, but when she saw who it was she gently laid her hand upon Yno's head, looked

The Beautiful Couple

at him long and sadly with great, hot tears dropping from her eyes, and then, with a smile infinitely more sad than her tears, she said in a gentle voice: "Yno! ask no questions, but if thy heart hath eyes thou wilt understand!" That evening she danced merrily, and when she went to bed she kissed her sister more lovingly than ever. Mora had a smile of wonderful gladness on her lips, and the hand that caressed her sister's hair seemed unaware of what it was touching. From that day the mild-faced Queen watched her daughters' faces with growing anxiety, and noticed that, whilst the one always grew happier, the other seemed to be continually striving to hide some consuming grief. Yet they would start for their rides together, and when they turned round to wave their hands to the royal couple on the balcony, the sun still seemed to be pouring down upon nothing but gladness. But when the forest was reached. Corona used quietly to rein in her golden-skinned Jorio, and with a sickening pain at her heart realized that the other two never even seemed to notice that she was no more at their side. Then she would turn her horse another way, and when she had reached a spot where violets grew like a purple carpet, she would slide from her saddle and hide her face amongst the delicate flowers, crushing their sweetness; and Jorio, with dumb affection, would stretch his long, silky neck and stir her hair with his snorting nostrils. And not far off Yno would remain silent behind the branches of a great tree, his face hidden in his hands. Sometimes, with a beating heart, he would come slowly nearer, and would lay his face on his mistress's small velvet clad feet, and kiss them softly, and then she would say, her voice smothered amongst the violets: "Yno! They never even notice when I am no more with them."

No, they noticed nothing but themselves, and one day, before the pool where they had met first, Ilario bent his head down from his tall horse and met Mora's upturned lips, and all the world was forgotten in the wonder of that first kiss. All the birds sang around them, and a nightingale lifted its sweet voice and sang its eternal song of love – that song so sweet to happy lovers, so unutterably sad to those who stand alone. And the little lizards on the ground came out to look at the beautiful couple, the butterflies, blue and yellow and snow-white, circled around them, and a great, brown-eyed gazelle peered timidly through the branches; even a little white hare forgot its usual fear, and sat up on its hind legs, craning its neck to see. Only the old eagle who had met them all three the first day flew silently away, and hovered long over the quiet figure that lay amongst the violets, and once again he was saddened by all the grief and the joy that the world contained side by side.

That night Ilario asked the King and Queen for the hand of their daughter Mora, and the King rejoiced and was glad; but the mother's heart was wrung at the thought of the one who was to be left behind. The ball that evening was more gorgeous than ever, and there were great rejoicings. The two sisters were clad in snow-white, with a girdle of pearls round their waists, and in their hair there were wreaths of white roses intertwined with pearls that hung down at each side of their heads. From their shoulders were suspended silver mantles, with golden rays worked upon them from the top, reaching down to the hem, and when they moved in the stately dance it seemed as if the sun were following them everywhere. Corona smiled with all the others, and was the first to bring her sister a beautiful gift – a small casket of sky-blue enamel encrusted with diamond crosses the colour of moon-rays; within it lay a tiny book, the cover of which was carved out of a huge, many-coloured opal, edged with tiny diamonds, and on its small ivory pages were inscribed in gold all the sayings that brought luck to those who read them, collected from every corner of the world by all the wise men ever known. As Corona laid the casket in her sister's hand, she kissed her on the eyes, and knew that with that kiss she was saying goodbye to all the days of their happy youth, of their perfect comradeship, and to all that had been, and never could be again. And Mora put her arms round her, and for one moment again all the world seemed to be concentrated in her twin sister, and she remembered how they had always sworn they could never part, and a sharp pain seemed to shoot across all her gladness. She, too, seemed suddenly to realize that the first page of her life was over; but Corona met her look with so brave a smile, so sweet, that the pain passed, and Mora turned once more in complete happiness to her lover.

When Mora was fast asleep, tired by all the rejoicings and festivities, Corona arose from her bed, which was close to her sister's, and, going to the window, sat down beside it, and looked far out over the moonlit sea. There she remained far into the night, with dry eyes, whilst her mother prayed for her below, and in the shade of a cypress-tree, hidden from his mistress's gaze, stood Yno, sobbing as if his heart would break.

The time for the wedding drew near, and Ilario's father, the old king from the mountainous country, sent wonderful gifts for his future daughter, being too ill to come himself and let her know how happy he was that his son had chosen so well. The happy day was drawing nigh, when suddenly a great terror came to them all: Ilario fell ill, and in spite of all the court doctors no one could discover what ailed him. Day and night he lay tossing on his bed in great pain, half conscious of all around him, and only finding peace when Mora laid her hand upon his burning forehead. But as the days passed he grew weaker and weaker. Once, when worn out by her long watches. Mora had gone to snatch a few minutes' sleep, she asked Corona to take her place. With a beating heart she took the low seat next his couch, straightened the pillow beneath his head, drew up the embroidered covering around him, then leant down and gazed long at the face she loved so well and hardly ever dared to look upon. Suddenly Ilario raised himself on one arm and opened his eyes wide, wide – oh, such beautiful eyes! – but they saw nothing, for fever was raging within his weakened body. Then he began uttering wild words of love, all for Mora, whom he imagined to be still beside him; and although Corona tried to silence him, it was useless; he became more and more excited, and Corona had at last to hold him in her arms to quiet him. Still he poured forth all his tenderness, and with a breaking heart she silently received the words of love which were meant for another. Long she sat after he had fallen asleep, his hand clasping her robe, and his burning head reposing upon her arm; and when Mora came back she was horrified to see the ghastly pallor of her sister's face.

The wedding-day came nearer and nearer, and still Ilario lay sick unto death. All the great doctors from all the countries of the world were called together; but all their learning seemed in vain, all their efforts, all their drugs and medicines were of no avail.

One day a gipsy came to the castle door and begged leave to enter. At first they would not give her admittance, but the Queen, who was looking from the tower window, saw her, and had her led up the great staircase to her own chamber, and there the gipsy told her, that far off, at the other side of the great forest, beyond a vast space of boggy waste, lived a wise woman; that she knew all the herbs of the universe, and that surely she could tell what would cure the sick Prince. The Queen listened attentively, and asked if the gipsy would go and fetch the wise woman; but the gipsy shook her head, and answered that she could not; that only a young girl, whose soul was as white as God's snow, could traverse the dangerous bog that lay between the forest and the witch's dwelling. At this the Queen felt sad; she called her daughters to her, and the gipsy repeated the tale to them. Hardly had she ended, when Corona sprang to her feet, and declared she would go to the witch's dwelling. Her mother and sister tried to dissuade her, in terror of all the dangers that would threaten her. But Corona would listen to no objections, and at last, with tears in their eyes, they gave way, after Corona had promised to ride Jorio and to take Yno with her as a companion. At daybreak she started. The sky was still red from the rising sun, which dazzled the eyes of her parents and Mora, who stood on the tower balcony to see the last of her. There they remained till she was but a small speck against the sun, and it seemed to them as if it were drawing her onward, to swallow her up in its great warmth. Yno followed her close behind, happy to be alone with her on her dangerous quest. But Corona was silent, and rode on without turning her head, and all the beauties of the forest seemed not to exist for her; the flowers beckoned to her in vain, in their shining beauty, in the glory of their many colours. The birds sang, but she heard them not; and all the animals who loved her well came out to greet her, but she heeded them not; with bent head she passed onward, silent, with eyes that seemed to notice nothing around her.

On she rode for many hours; even the beauty of Jorio, who seemed to send out rays of light from his shining neck, brought no smile to her lips, and Yno felt with a pang that she had quite forgotten his presence. She rode all day, and till now no hindrance and no difficulty barred her way, but towards sunset she came to the border of the marshy land she was to cross in order to reach the wise woman's dwelling. This bit of land stood in bad repute, and the desolation of its aspect froze her heart and courage within her. It seemed to consist of a greyish slime, in which the skeletons of trees rose gaunt and yellow like bleached bones; some had colourless lichens hanging from them, like hair on an old woman's corpse. Evening shadows were already spreading over the dread place, and seemed to move like the ghosts of tormented souls that could find no rest. The bank that led down was steep, and an evil smelling water oozed out like oil between the withered grass. Yno had sprung from his horse, and came up to his Princess's side, looking with anxious eyes into her face.

"Sweet mistress, do not go!" he cried; "thy horse will not carry thee across that horrible swamp; he will sink and drag thee with him."

Jorio gave a scream of pain and terror. Corona slowly turned her head to Yno, and gently, like one in a dream, answered:

"Yno, I must go, and alone!"

"No! no!" cried Yno; "that must not be. I shall at least die at thy side!"

"Yno," repeated Corona, "I must go alone; make not my task more hard! I am weary, and the heart I bear within me weighs me to the ground. Yno! Yno! Obey and hinder me not!"

And Yno submitted, and lifted her from her horse in his strong arms. She noticed not the tender adoration of his touch. Once more she turned to him:

"Yno, wait for me here; I shall return in safety, because it is for another I go, and God will bless my quest!"

Then she laid her head a moment against Jorio's neck, and kissed him between his dilated nostrils. "Jorio, you also must await me here," she whispered. "I shall come back!" Then she slid down the ugly bank, and Yno sank upon his knees, his hands folded in prayer, his eyes wide open, following with an agony of anxiety her figure, now hardly distinguishable in the growing dark. But suddenly he noticed that round her head there shone a white light like a halo, and that her steps did not sink into the grey slime, and he remembered the gipsy's words: "Only a young girl whose soul is as white as God's snow can cross the dangerous bog." "Her soul is white," murmured Yno to himself – "white as God's snow, and God has put a saint's halo round her head to guide her steps"; and he cried as if his heart would break. But Corona's soul, in spite of her outward calm, was full of that nameless terror which comes to all young creatures when they are alone in the dark; and the shadows flitting around her froze her blood with awe and fear. She would have cried aloud if she had not remembered Yno on the bank, who would have tried to follow her. Sometimes the skeletons of the trees in the ghastly light appeared to her like threatening figures barring her way. But she thought of Ilario lying on his bed, sick unto death, and she drew her long, blue cloak around her, and pressed onward, her feet growing wearier from the effort of walking through the sickening slime, which clogged her steps and seemed to freeze the life within her. Once it seemed to her that she saw the figure of a man before her, with a bleeding heart, into which a dagger was thrust, and that the blood dripped down, making a red pool on the grey mud; but the horrible figure vanished, to be replaced by the crouching figure of a woman, who held a dead

The Bog

child in her arms; the child's head hung over the side of the woman's lap, and its hair dabbled in the slime on the ground. Corona cried out at last in an anguish of horror, but only her own voice seemed to echo again and again in the drear silence, and the woman's figure also vanished. Then it seemed to her that out of the darkness cold hands were touching her face, and the breath of unseen things stirred her hair. The sweat of fear stood on her forehead, but she still pressed onward. Suddenly she saw a vision of three young girls, with their arms stretched out towards her, and all three, instead of eyes, had gaping holes, out of which snakes were creeping with a hideous, slow, sliding movement. And when they in their turn disappeared, she suddenly came upon the body of a man hung on one of the gaunt trees, and his eyes seemed still alive, and showed an agony no words could describe. Then Corona sank on her knees and hid her head in the cloak; she felt the cold night wind freezing her very bones, and for a moment she thought her mind would give way. There was a hideous sound of wailing all around her, and sudden screams and hoarse whispers; a hand seemed to touch her; she raised her head sharply, and saw what looked like the shadow of a man slinking away, with something terrible hidden beneath his cloak. Corona sank on the ground, and drew her hair round her face, wrapping herself within its golden masses, to shut out all sound and all vision, and for a long time she lay there like one dead, and the awful shadows flitted around her, but none dared harm her, because of the halo she wore all unconsciously round her head. For hours she lay thus, quite unable to rise, worn out by the sadness of her heart, the fear around her, and the exhaustion of tramping through the mire, that tried at each of her steps to draw her beneath its surface; besides, she had taken no food since she left her father's palace.

The grey dawn grew out of the fearful darkness, and a pale gleam of light lit up the horizon. Corona once more raised her head, and her golden hair fell away like great sunlit waves from her face, which looked out between them like the face of a drowned corpse, her eyes wide open with the fear of all she had seen. All her blood seemed to have left her body, blanching even her lips. But suddenly thought came back to her clearly, and with it the vision of Ilario dying, whom she had gone forth to save. She stretched both hands up to Heaven, and in a great cry she called to God to give her fresh courage; then she struggled to her feet, and noticed to her relief that a new day was dawning, and that with the coming light the drear shadows had gone to rest. The great waste of quagmire stood out horrible in all its loneliness, and the stretch before her was covered with stripes of ghastly mist, that seemed alive and as if moved about by some restless misery. But the hideous visions had gone, and once more she pressed forward, her beautiful clothes torn and soiled, her blue cloak bordered with mud and discoloured by the greyish slime. One of her golden shoes had been sucked from her foot, which was bleeding, and the other had lost all shape. But she heeded not her pain and fatigue, but struggled onward, the love in her heart giving her the strength she needed. Thus she wandered on and on during the whole of the next day; and besides all her other fears she was afraid of what she was going to find when she reached the witch. Would she help her? Would she send her away? Would she be like the awful shadows of the night? Would she be cruel and hard with her and ill-use her, now that her strength was nearly all gone?

Suddenly she saw before her the sea! Oh, the sea! Her sea! Surely her troubles must end, now that the sea was once more before her eyes! The sea with all its sweet recollections! And in a rush all the happy visions of her childhood and youth rose before her, and once more she sat in their golden boat, beneath the purple sail with its proud emblem, and once more Mora's hand was in hers, and all the pain of the last months seemed but a dream. She heard Mora's happy voice telling her the tales that made her laugh, and saw the kind faces of her parents, bent down towards them from the upper terrace, as they landed. And she saw the golden steps that resembled Jacob's ladder, and smelt the sweet perfume of the roses that grew in coloured masses over the balustrade, on which her father and mother were leaning. . . . With a start she came back to reality, and once more all the aching fatigue took possession of her; wearily she sank upon a great stone, searching with her eyes all around her, and it seemed to her that not far off there was an old boat on the beach, lying on the white sand, like the body of a whale. The shadows were thickening, and she said to herself, wearily, that she had probably missed her way, and that in spite of having passed all the horrors of the swamp, she had not found what she was seeking. Once more, with her failing strength, she raised herself, feeling, that if she were to die, she would rather die beneath the shade of the kindly, forsaken-looking boat. She dragged herself slowly, slowly towards the battered vessel, and just as she reached it, all her life seemed to go from her, and she fell forward on the sand, her long hair streaming down towards the incoming tide. When she came to herself once more, she found herself in a small, dark room, a single candle burning beside her; and all around her were fishing-nets, and shells the colour of butterflies on the shelves and walls; and a wonderful bunch of strange tinted seaweed was on a small table, in a bowl of rarest workmanship. Beside the bowl lay an old leather-bound book, and on the book shone a pearl, of wondrous size and beauty, the like of which Corona had never seen, even in her father's treasury. All this she realized as in a strange dream, and with her returning faculties she also began to feel once more all the pain of her weary body, and all the ache of her heavy heart.

A door opened softly, and a strange woman came towards her where she lay – a woman with a face so sad, that Corona thought she had never seen anything so sad before. She was dressed in a plain black dress of the roughest stuff, and her head was shrouded in a thick, black veil, that hung to the ground like a cloak. Her colourless face was still young, but Corona noticed that her hair was snow-white, as if it had been bleached by some sudden grief. Encircling her neck, she wore a short string of wonderful pearls, round and white, and shining as if alive with secret life; but they seemed in glaring contrast to the poor clothing and surroundings. The woman bent her face to Corona, and laid a strong white hand on her aching brow, and all the pain seemed to be drawn from her into the long, finely shaped fingers, and once more Corona felt that life and vigour were beginning to stream through her body, so that she raised herself on the couch and sat up. Till then neither had spoken, and now Corona, her eyes fixed on the strange woman, said in a whisper:

"Who art thou?" And the woman answered:

"I am the wise woman thou hast come to seek. I am the witch, at the thought of whom thy heart beat with fear; but before we talk drink this, for thou hast come far and thy feet are weary, and thou hast taken no food for two days." And she gave her a small bowl, of some curious white stone, and held it to Corona's lips, and she drank gratefully. The taste of what she drank was strange and sweet, an unknown taste, which refreshed her and made her feel strong once more, so that she wished to rise to her feet. But the wise woman pressed her gently back on the bed, and said, in a voice that sounded like the distant moan of the sea:

"Now tell me thy quest!"

And Corona told her about Ilario's illness, and how all the doctors had failed, and what the gipsy had said; then she joined her hands in prayer, and hot tears gushed from her eyes, and she begged the wise woman to give her a cure for the sick man.

"Be still, fair child!" answered the woman; "long ago my heart died within me, and I have no more tears to shed; the sea cries for me now; I have heard her voice, and she is my only friend. Yet I am wise, and though dead and broken my heart can feel the pain of others!" And then, turning to the table, and taking from it the old book, upon which the wonderful pearl lay, she put the pearl gently down, and opened the book.

"See here," she continued, "this book was once brought me from a distant land; it came from far over the sea, and within its pages lies all the wisdom of the World. With its help I can tell thee what thou must do."

And as she spoke she turned over the yellow, faded leaves with her marble-white hands, and bringing the candle nearer she bent her head, her shadow was large and still against the wall behind her, and the light gleamed upon the snow of her hair, turning it to gold once more, so that Corona seemed to see her as she must have been before – before what? Corona did not know, but she felt that she was in the presence of some great grief.

The woman raised her head, and her eyes had a far-away look; and in a monotonous voice, as if recalling some chant of other days, she spoke:

The Wise Woman

"In a far-off country, which can be reached only by one person quite alone, who has made the promise of utter silence during all her wanderings, there stands in the middle of a strange and awful forest, inhabited by cruel beasts, a temple of snow-white marble, composed of six separate courts, each guarded by a different kind of wild beast. In the sixth and innermost court of all there lies a pool of dark water, and in the midst of the pool grows the Lily of Life; its whiteness is so intense, that human eye cannot look upon it without becoming blind. He who wishes to pick the Lily of Life is in danger of being drowned in the water, or blinded by the flower; but he who succeeds in plucking it can heal any illness, stop any torment, cure any madness. So saith the wisest of books." The woman's voice stopped, and she looked before her, as in a trance, whilst Corona, with beating heart and eager eyes, listened, listened. The woman did not move, and Corona, at last, stretched out her hand and gently touched her.

"Oh, tell me how I can get there!" she whispered.

The wise woman replied, still looking straight before her, without turning her head:

"Is he thy lover?"

"No!" cried Corona, with a cry of pain. At that the woman turned and looked deep into her eyes.

"And yet thou wouldst go?"

"Oh, yes, for Mora's sake!"

"Is, then, the love for a sister so great?" Then Corona bent her face to her knees and sobbed.

"Say no more!" came the soft, far-off voice, "say no more! I will help thee; thou shalt find the Lily of Life; but thy courage must be great, and thy will must be firm, and thou must never, however sorely tempted, open thy lips to speak, or answer any question put to thee. Thou must go alone, quite alone, and thou must not cry out in pain, if hurt; no sound of complaint must escape thy lips, and even if afraid thou must utter no sound."

Corona listened, breathless; she thought of her awful wandering across the marsh, and her heart felt sick within her; but all she said was: "I thank thee, kind mother! I will do thy bidding; but is it not a quest above the strength of a simple maid like me?"

"No," answered the woman, "because thy heart is pure, and the love that burns within thee is no selfish love: I will help thee." And she turned to a small cupboard in the wall, and as she did so Corona noticed for the first time that the room she lay in was the inside of a boat! She gazed around her and saw on all sides strange things that reminded her of the sea, and a great curiosity came over her to know who the woman was, for she felt that some strange history lay behind those eyes and in that voice that had taken the sound of the moaning sea.

"Kind mother! Tell me, prithee, who thou art," said Corona, rising from the bed and putting her hand on the woman's shoulder, "and tell me why they call thee the witch, when thy heart is so tender. Tell me, because I feel that my heart yearns towards thee, and because all sad women are my sisters!"

The strange woman paused where she stood, lifted her head and gazed through the tiny window, although all was black outside, and nothing but the restless sea was to be heard.

"My voice has lost all human sound; I have lived alone for many years, because I carry an awful sin in my heart," she replied, in her toneless voice, "but unto thee I will speak, because my soul knoweth thy pain, and although I can love no more, as my heart is dead, I can pity those who suffer. Listen!"

As she said the last words, she unwound the black veil from her head, and as she did so her hair streamed all over her, snow-white, in great foaming waves, and she suddenly seemed quite young, and a mysterious beauty lit up her sad features. From the table she took the wonderful pearl, and held it between her fingers with an infinite tenderness; then she began to speak:

"Thou seest me old, because my hair is white; once it was as thine, passing fair; my face was young and fresh as the opening rose; but it is not age that has blanched my hair – it is grief! It is not the weight of years that has wiped out the bloom from my cheeks – it is tears! I loved a fisher-lad, but I was proud, and pretended to play with his love, and because of my wondrous beauty he was my slave, and I said unto him: 'Fetch me pearls from the bottom of the sea, pearls to wear round my neck!' At first he came back from his wanderings and brought no pearls – he brought me yonder strange and beautiful bowl of gold and precious stones, and those strange coloured sea-weeds that it contains. He dived deep, in unheard-of places, through awful danger, to bring them to me, but I was not content. He brought me that bowl from which thou drankest, – a strange treasure from an Indian temple, once thrown into the sea by an angry priest; and he brought me these glowing, coloured shells; but I said I would have pearls – pearls the tears of the sea – pearls more wondrous than any king possessed, to wear them round my throat. So he dived always deeper, and in more dangerous spots, and after each journey he brought me a pearl. Now, behold, I have forty pearls more beautiful than any thy father possesses; they are white as snow, and yet each seems alive with living blood! But still I was not content, and I wept, saying I desired to possess a pearl larger than any yet known, and my lover was sad because the years passed, and I was never satisfied. Yet I loved him well, but the youth within me was proud and wicked, and those around me called me the witch, because of the power I had through my beauty. I was tempted to misuse it.

"On a glorious summer's morn my lover started once more, and before he left I kissed him on the lips, and said that on his return with the pearl I would become his wife. And his face was glad; and I stood on the shore and waved my golden hair to him till he disappeared over the shining waves. When he was quite out of sight, I sat down on a rock and sang a song of wild triumph, so sure was I that he would return with the pearl I had wished for. But one awful morning the storm-tossed sea cast up his boat, and within it he lay, cold, white, and dead. Between his hands he held a great pearl – a pearl of such wondrous size and beauty as no man had ever seen – and in his eyes the tears were frozen into sparkling diamonds, and curious, coloured seaweeds clung to his clothes; and his face was sad, sad with a wondering look upon it, as if he still had a question left unanswered." The woman paused and drew her white hair over her face, and then slowly, very slowly, she once more spoke:

"For three days I lay upon his body to try to warm life back into him, but in vain; and when at last they lifted me from him my hair was as white as it is now! And we buried him out there, beneath the great rock, and all the sea-birds came and sat upon his grave. I made my home in his old boat, and have lived here ever since, surrounded by the things he gave me. For many years I did nothing but sit by the sea, in all weathers, quite close to his grave, my hands folded in my lap, and my hair swept backwards and forwards like sea-foam in the storm. One day an old man came to me – who he was I do not know – but he had come from far. He had known and loved my dear one, and he put this book into my hand, saying: 'Make amends for thy sin by being useful to others! Here in this book thou shalt find all the wisdom of the East and West; give all thy mind to it, and become a blessing unto others, as thou hast been a curse unto him that loved thee!' He left me, and from that day I have done as he bade me, and now people call me the wise woman or the witch, because of my great knowledge." The white-haired woman paused, and the one candle threw weird lights on her tall figure; in her pale hands she held the old book, and they seemed to touch its faded pages tenderly.

"Now this pearl always lies on the book," she continued dreamily, "reminding me of my wisdom and my folly."

Her eyes seemed to seek something far away, and her voice became more than ever like the moan of the sea. For a while neither spoke, but Corona had taken hold of the sad woman's hand, and laid it against her cheek. Outside the wind howled, and the seagulls' screams were like the voices of drowning men. Corona shuddered, but then gave her whole attention to the low voice of the woman, who turned to her, and said:

"Now I will give thee what thou needest for thy painful wanderings"; and she opened the small cupboard and laid three things in Corona's hands – a curious piece of metal, which she called a magnet, and which she explained would draw the wanderer always towards the place she was seeking, so that she must follow it blindly wherever it led, however difficult the road; a little strangely shaded lamp that would light of itself when she needed help; and a round piece of yellow glass, which she was to hold before her eyes, so as to be able to approach the Lily, which otherwise would blind her. Corona took the wise woman's hand and kissed it, saying:

"May God bless thee for thy help; may the good action bring back a little gladness to thy heart; but one more question: I pray thee now tell me if I must return over the fearful swamp. And may I go a moment to my father's castle to tell my sister of the hope I have to help her? and then" – here Corona bent her head low, and her voice became but a whisper – "I wish to gaze once more – before I go; I should have more courage if –"

Her voice choked, and she leant her face against the door of the cabin.

"Thou canst go by sea to thy father's castle, and I will send a seagull to tell thy faithful follower, Yno, to await thee on the beach. But only at night must thou enter the castle, when all are sleeping; and thou shalt not speak with any one, but here is a message for thy sister; it will tell her that her heart may hope, and," gently added the woman, "do not awake those that sleep, not even if it would make thy going easier; no one must know why thou goest, nor what force sustains thee – dost understand?" And she laid her hand on Corona's shoulder, and looked at her gravely, with sad eyes that seemed to have concentrated within them all the gazing of those who search without finding. "I shall watch over thy wanderings; and when thou deemst thyself most forsaken, then will my thoughts be with thee. Depart with courage; I will take thee to my boat."

They descended to the seashore, where a small boat stood tied to an old post.

"My boat will take thee the right way. God be with thee; and in thy tears for thyself weep also for me, who have no more tears to shed!"

Corona sprang into the boat, clasping within her hands the magnet, the little lamp, and the yellow glass. The strange woman stood tall and straight on the seashore, like the statue of grief, without a movement either of farewell or encouragement, whilst the waves took possession of the boat, and carried Corona far out, so that the woman's silent figure soon became but a speck in the distance.

All day the boat moved of itself, and Corona watched the sun gradually change its place. It was only as night fell that she suddenly discovered her father's castle standing out, a dark mass against the sky. Her whole being seemed to call for those days for ever past, when she had been a happy child at Mora's side, and when each awakening day had contained a world of joy! On the beach stood Yno, his faithful face all lit up; but Corona laid her finger on her lips, and made him understand that she must pronounce not a word. Then slowly and noiselessly she began to ascend the long golden stairs between the two lines of dark cypresses, and it seemed to her as if all the familiar things had become strange, like things only seen in a dream and vaguely remembered. She pressed her hands over her golden hair, wondering if it had turned as white as the wise woman's. Slowly, slowly, she mounted the stairs, and never had her limbs seemed less elastic; never had the beautiful steps seemed to her so endless. All was dark and quiet within the castle, but for fear of being seen, Corona waited long beneath a dark tree, so as to slip into the house when all were sleeping. Suddenly the window of her mother's room opened, and she saw her mother looking wistfully across the sea, in the direction of the place whence Corona had started. She noticed that her face looked worn, and that she folded her hands as if in prayer. Corona longed to rush forward and cry out that she was there, to be taken into those kind arms, and to give way like a little child to all her grief. But she remembered her vow of silence, and smothered the words that rose to her lips, pressing her face against the rough bark of a tree to resist the almost overwhelming temptation to ask for help in her trouble. The friendly window closed once more, and all again was still.

After a little while Corona slipped into the silent castle, and with infinite precautions she contrived, without being seen, to reach the room where Ilario was lying ill. She softly opened the door, and in the half light of the room she found her sister asleep with her head on Ilario's feet; but the sick man's eyes were wide open with the terrible fever which had his body in its grasp. Corona's heart beat so fast that she had to lean against the wall, so as not to fall. Her knees seemed to give way beneath her, and her pulses to be throbbing in her eyes. She was afraid she might awaken the sleeping Mora, because to her all the room seemed filled with the sound of her heart-throbs. On her knees she dragged herself to the bed, and then a fearful longing came over her. Once, only once, she must – yes, she must put her lips to his; once before she went to bring him life, for another. – Surely God would not punish her for this! She would bear all if she could have but that one supreme happiness! She bent her head down – oh, so softly! And the sick man seemed to smile at her, and then for a short, wonderful moment she pressed her lips to his burning ones. Then Corona was filled with a nameless terror; she hastily rose, leaving the wise woman's message between her sleeping sister's fingers. Then, noiselessly, like a thief, she left the room, the castle, and rushed blindly down the long stairs of gold, as if afraid of her own thoughts. When she reached the shore, she saw the witch's boat still there. She sprang into it, with only one thought – to get away, away, far from temptation, and begin all her terrible wanderings. As the boat left the shore, she saw Yno come rushing down the old stairs, like a shadow in the dark night, and to her horror she saw him dash into the sea, just as he was, to try to reach her boat, which was already drifting rapidly away. Then the sudden fear came to her that he would be drowned; she did not know how to stop the boat, because the magnet was already drawing it far away, in the direction that she had to go. With all her soul she prayed that the boat might pause a moment. She cried to the distant wise woman:

"Let not that faithful heart perish! Let me not add that horror to the burden I already bear!" Then the boat stopped suddenly, and Yno's head appeared as a speck in the water. After what seemed an endless time he reached the boat, clambered in, and poured out a torrent of words. Corona was afraid he would die, such was his breathless exhaustion. But through it all she remembered her vow of silence, and although the despairing youth besought her to return, or to allow him to come with her, she kept her fingers on her lips, and shook her head.

How could she make him understand that she must go alone, and that no companion must share her lonely wanderings? How could she induce him to leave her? The boat began to move again, and Corona felt that it was impossible to abandon him once more to the waves, so she decided in her mind to let him lie at her feet till the boat reached some shore. She drew her cloak round him, as he lay shivering, his arms clasping her knees, and she could not help a feeling of comfort to know him there, to feel his living, breathing form close against her, to guess at the faithful look in his eyes in that sad, dark night. He had given up questioning her, when he found that for some reason she could not or would not answer him, and lay there like a faithful dog, guarding her with all his jealous devotion, little

The Sick Prince

understanding what a difficulty his presence caused, and how she was pondering in what way she could make him understand that he must not follow her. By degrees his gasping breath became calmer, and she noticed that he had dropped into a peaceful sleep. But Corona sat straight and still, her eyes fixed on the darkness, with the vision always before her eyes of the sick man on his bed of suffering, and of her sister lying with her head on his feet.

At daybreak they reached a shore which looked desolate enough, and there the boat ran into the sand as if drawn by invisible hands. Yno lifted Corona out, and then came the moment when she had to make him understand that he must leave her. She noticed that he was watching her anxiously. At last she decided to write on the sand with a sharp stone: "Follow me not, for I must go alone. Obey me, else will all my weary toil be of no avail. If thou lovest me, make it not hard for me." So once more, with a breaking heart, he saw her go; this time over a bleached, desert-like plain, where the sun seemed to beat down, mercilessly devouring all that tried to grow. But there was no doubt that the magnet was drawing Corona farther and farther over that burning plain. She walked on and on, regardless of the scorching sun, and stumbling against the rolling stones that lay everywhere. There was no tree to be seen, no path, no comfortable shade, no green blade of grass to refresh the eye. On, on she wandered, till she felt almost faint with the pain of her bleeding feet and the terrible thirst that was torturing her. The hopelessness of it was, that she could see no end to this awful plain; only in the far distance rose great mountains, like those one sees in a painting, with the feeling that they are only there as a background. All of a sudden she heard the sound of wings, and a tiny little brown bird flew towards her and settled on her shoulder. An indescribable feeling of comfort came to the poor girl at this little living creature seeking shelter near her, on this wide plain where she had seemed the only living being. Then the little brown bird began to sing – oh! in such a heart-melting way, with a voice of such exquisite beauty, that Corona felt as if all her fatigue were leaving her, and new life were coming to her from an unknown source. That exquisite song! it contained in its notes all that her heart must keep silent, all the promise of future happiness, all the pictures of her sweet childhood, all the peace and beauty that might be. And whilst the little brown bird sang, she seemed to walk much quicker, and at last the mountains that had looked quite out of her reach came nearer. But the sun was sinking, and Corona felt that she must take some rest, or she would be unable to go farther. Besides, she had eaten nothing since she had left the witch's boathouse, and she knew that she must die of starvation if no help came to her. The little brown bird had flown away, and as the marvellous little voice died down in the distance. Corona once more felt all her weakness. She sank to the ground wearily, beside a grey rock, great dizziness came over her, though she tried to shake it off, and a curious feeling of faintness, as if her life were slipping from her little by little, as water leaks from a cracked vessel. She made an effort to keep her consciousness, but in vain; her head dropped, and all became dark around her. When she opened her eyes again, she could at first remember nothing, and she knew not how long she had been unconscious, but it seemed to her that she was no more there, in the great burning plain, though she was still too weak to sit up and look.

Suddenly she heard the sweet voice of the little bird, singing! singing! Oh, the joy of that sweet song! Did some kind angel send her the little bird, to keep her from despair? What was the magic power in that bird's voice, to make her feel life coming back each time it sang? She sat up, and all around her she saw a shady wood, where the sunshine filtered golden-yellow through the leaves. She rubbed her eyes – yes! she was not dreaming; quite close by ran a little crystal stream. Corona bent down towards it, and putting her lips to the water quenched her thirst. It seemed to her that never before had anything tasted so good, and then to her intense relief she saw some great melons close by. Oh, such a grand feast they were! And all the time she wondered how she had got to this place during her sleep or her faint. Had the magnet drawn her there? She now felt that it was urging her forward once more; so she rose to her feet, much refreshed, and walked on as fast as she could. This time her way lay along the clear little stream, and the moss growing along side was soft to walk on. But by degrees it seemed to her as if the air were getting much colder, and soon she noticed that the moss beneath her feet had been touched by frost, and looked withered and brown. Also the wood became thinner, till at last she was in the open once more; the little stream was becoming bigger, and instead of moss now beneath her feet there were stones; the stones grew larger and rougher, and the air became still colder. Soon the water in the stream froze, and a cold wind blew her hair about and made her shiver. On she pressed, the magnet always dragging her forward. Her limbs now were numb with cold, and her breath was visible like clouds of smoke that hung in the air, and remained frozen like a white haze on her hair and clothes. She felt an intolerable pain over all her body, and her feet were so cold, that each time they hit against a stone she almost cried aloud. But her courage did not give way, even in her half-conscious state. She wondered what sort of force sustained her, and once more all her past life unfurled in beautiful visions before her eyes, and she felt as if the Corona of then and now were two separate beings; one a vision in an impossible dream of happiness, and the other a creature on whom all the pain of the world hung heavily. On, on she stumbled; around her the country became more desolate, the air colder, till each breath she drew seemed to cut her lungs like a knife. On, on, but her steps became more lagging, and the pain caused by the cold and fatigue was intolerable. Suddenly the aspect of her surroundings changed, and she saw before her an immense frozen lake, dark and terrible, overhung by tremendous black rocks that dropped straight into it on all sides like great walls. And colder and colder grew the air, so that the tears of pain that came to her eyes froze against her cheeks.

"I can bear no more!" she whispered; "I shall die of fatigue, and cold, and pain. And to die would be a relief. Oh, dear God above! Let me die!" But no answer came from any side, only fearful silence all around; nothing breathed except herself. Suddenly a shadow fell before her, the great shadow of a man, and such a terror seized Corona, that all that had gone before seemed as nothing in comparison. She had not the courage to turn round, and held back the shriek that came to her throat. Each time she moved the shadow moved also; she felt as if some devil were following her, some spirit out of a terrible, unknown world. But as her foot reached the ice of the lake she stopped a moment, not daring to trust herself upon its shining surface. Before her stretched the dangerous sheet of ice; behind her lurked that nameless terror. Like a hunted animal she crouched down and hid her face in her cloak. Suddenly she felt a touch on her shoulder, and with all the courage that remained to her she turned round. Above her stood an old man, all frozen he seemed, like the country round; his great beard was covered with icicles, and on his head he wore a wide felt hat, that shaded his face. His hands, and what was to be seen of his face, were blue from the frost. His eyes

The Little Brown Bird

were deep-sunk and had a cruel look, his mouth twitched, as if with curses.

"What doest thou here in my region? How darest thou come and disturb my eternal silence? By what right does thy foot awaken echoes in this place of the forgotten? See here!" – and the man pointed to a place where a great number of rocks, all about the same size, gleamed in the cold light. "Look closer!" he ordered. "Those are not rocks – they are the bodies of all who disturbed my eternal rest with their voices and their echoing steps!"

Corona then saw that indeed each rock had a human form, and when she came nearer she noticed that the faces were ghastly, all expressing the same terrible longing to be free.

"Answer me," continued the man. "Why hast thou come here?"

Corona made no reply, but gazed up at him, and then pointed across the frozen lake, and each time the man pressed her to speak she only pointed towards the lake.

"Aha! Thou hast no voice – that is good for thee! For, above all, it is the human voice I cannot bear! But I shall let thee go where thou wouldst, because thine eyes have a look I have never seen before; nevertheless thou must pay me! For it is not only thine eyes that I fancy, but also thy wonderful hair, that has the colour of the sun, which I never see! Give me thy hair, and thou shalt go free."

Corona obediently bent her beautiful head, and with a few rough slashes of his knife the man severed the golden treasure, and it lay like ripe corn at her feet.

"Out of this I shall make myself a nest to keep me warm, but thou wilt be the colder!" And he laughed an awful, mirthless laugh, that echoed all around the mountains.

Corona certainly felt a strange feeling without her mantle of golden hair, and the cold bit more cruelly without its warm protection. But the dreadful man picked up the beautiful shining mass, twisted it like a muff round his blue hands, and went away still laughing.

The magnet became more insistent, and Corona, looking like some beautiful page-boy, now that her long hair was gone, at last ventured on the ice. As she did so, a peculiar whirring sound came from all sides, and she was surrounded by innumerable strange birds, all snow-white; many of them seized Corona's blue cloak, and she felt herself gliding softly across the mirror-like ice, as if she had been on skates. The birds were all round her, preventing her from falling, forming a great chair with their snowy wings, supporting her back, and screening her from the cutting blasts of the wind. Corona gave herself up to their care, with a feeling of sweet relief, and as in a swift sledge she was borne away towards the great wall of mountains that rose almost black at the end of the lake. When they reached it, the birds circled once or twice round her with curious, sad shrieks, as if loth to leave her; but gradually they began to fly higher and higher, till they seemed like a snowstorm far up in the air. Corona wondered what was to come next, because, in spite of the bitter cold, which still froze her limbs, she felt more rested. Suddenly the magnet gave a jerk upwards in her hand. Corona gazed at the barrier before her, and realized that in that black wall of rock there were steps – steps cut into the stone, that lay one above the other, perpendicularly, and led up, up, up farther than eye could see. What! Was she to climb that awful staircase? Up that wall of rock, where a single slip would mean certain death upon the ice beneath? Up that fearful wall, where there was nothing to cling to except the next step? She could not! She could not! With her aching feet and frozen fingers she could not! She almost wished the dreadful man had turned her into a rock like the others who had tried to come the same way as she.

Then suddenly it seemed to her as if a vision passed before her eyes; she saw Ilario as he had been that first day of their meeting by the pool, in his golden, gleaming armour, young and healthy; and then she saw him fever-stricken on his bed of suffering, and she knew that she would face that awful ascent. With a prayer for God's help she mounted the first step, the second – the third – up, up; soon she was far above the frozen lake. Her feet were bleeding, her hands could hardly feel the stone to which they clung. She dared not look up or down, but kept her face pressed close to the rock, so as to see nothing of the fearful depth yawning beneath her, which, with each step, grew greater. But all the same a great feeling of sickness was coming over her; she knew her strength was failing; and like one drowning she saw all her life over again in vivid flashes. Yet the magnet drew her on, on. Each step seemed now more impossible to take, and on each she had to rest long, her face pressed against the next step, incapable of moving, feeling ill with horror and despair. She knew that her strength was ebbing fast, but that all would soon be over, and that her end was near. The instinct of self-preservation was all that still remained to her, and gave her mutilated hands the power to cling on.

But what was that? Was she dreaming? No! The flutter of tiny wings, and then a voice so sweet, so heavenly sweet, so exquisite, that it penetrated every fibre of her being! And a soft, brown, little body was close against her cheek. Oh, that sweet song! So full of a happiness that was no more hers. But that so took possession of her, that all physical sensations seemed to exist no more. That brave little voice sent forth all its perfection of sound, and Corona, quite unconsciously, climbed higher and higher. The nearer the top she came, the warmer was the air, and the sweeter did the little brown bird sing. It seemed to have many souls, all of which it expressed in its heavenly song. Corona stretched out her hand to find another step, but – oh, was it possible? Her hand met a broad, smooth surface. She opened her eyes – could it be true? Was it not some terrible fantastic vision? Could it be that she had reached the top of that fearful wall of rock? A last great effort, that made her feel her life was going from her, and she was really over the edge, and the frozen lake below seemed like a far-off well of darkness. Corona shut her eyes, and remained lying flat on the ground, all her strength spent, shuddering with the fearful realization of what she had escaped. Her feet and hands were bleeding, her clothes were torn, her hair no longer protected her neck from the cold, all her body was bruised, and the pain she felt was such, that her only longing was to die – to die, never to have to lift her head again. But the little brown bird wished it otherwise. It came quite near, and brushing her bent head with its soft feathers, it began its song again. It sang with the voice of all that is beautiful in the world – a voice such as one hopes that the angels will have. Although Corona was too weak to move, that song comforted her as nothing else could comfort her, and the sun looked down upon her prostrate form, and sent out his warmest rays to thaw her frozen limbs. So strong were his beams, that little strawberry plants near by unfurled their leaves, disclosing bunches of beautiful red fruit, that hung like shining little drops of blood on their thin stalks. And the little brown bird continued to sing, sing; and whilst it sang Corona fell into a deep sleep. She slept many hours, and when she awoke the sun had done his work well, and she felt warm at last. She sat up, and found the beautiful strawberries, which refreshed her, but she

The Frozen Lake

longed for something more sustaining, she felt so weak and hungry. The magnet was beginning to draw her on again. She noticed that she was on a very high plateau with a wonderful view, far up over the terrible lake. She could look over the mountains into other valleys which faded away into a hazy blue.

"I must be very high up," she said to herself, "because I seem to overlook all the world; but I wonder where the Lily lies; I wonder if I shall ever get there! And if I get there, shall I be in time? And how shall I get back with the precious flower?" And a great feeling of discouragement overwhelmed her. She looked at her wounded feet, her lacerated hands, her torn clothes, felt her head shorn of its glorious gold; then she burst into tears. Like a little child she sobbed as if her heart would break, but the magnet left her no peace; it began dragging her on towards a far-off forest. She was seized by a sudden terror lest perhaps she had lost the little lamp and the yellow glass. She felt in her pocket – no, they were there, quite safe; she struggled to her feet; she was in great pain, and could move but slowly.

After about an hour's very slow progress, she saw, with a throb of pleasure, a tiny house hidden under a great shady tree. She approached it noiselessly and with great hesitation, feeling that she could no more find the strength to meet cruel faces or angry words. She crept up cautiously to the little window; within sat two men by a fire, cooking something in a pot. One man was middle-aged, the other was quite young, and had a handsome face and long brown curls that fell upon his shoulders. Both men were clad in rough leather clothes with large belts, and each had an axe. "Wood-cutters," thought Corona. "They look rough, but perhaps their hearts will be compassionate and they will let me rest, and perhaps even give me a little of their food"; so very nervously she knocked at the door. It was immediately opened, and the young man stood before her. She was just going to ask for their hospitality, when she remembered her vow of silence, so she stood there with bent head, her hands raised in supplication. She was so beautiful, in spite of the sorry plight she was in, that the young man stepped back with a gesture of wonder.

"Strange maiden, whence comest thou?" he asked, beckoning her to enter. But Corona shook her head sadly, and put her hand to her mouth to indicate that she was dumb.

The older man had also risen, and in a rough but not unkind voice demanded:

"What seekest thou of us in this poor hut?"

Again Corona shook her head, pointing to her wounded feet, her torn hands and clothes, making them understand that she was weary, weary unto death! The young man led her to a bed of skins in the corner, and all the time he kept gazing at her beautiful face; and shyly and with wonder he touched the tissue of her dark blue cloak, the torn but beautiful under-dress, and the golden belt round her waist. But when he saw the state of her bleeding feet he brought a rough, wooden basin, and very gently, with his awkward hands, bathed her feet in cold water, which made her wince with pain. And whilst his son was making himself thus useful, the old woodcutter tried to make Corona talk, but all in vain. He told her that he and his son were woodmen of the forest yonder, a great and endless forest, to the middle of which no one had quite penetrated as yet; but that he and his boy earned a living by cutting wood on its outskirts. That though poor, they were contented, but in winter in constant danger, because of all the wild animals that lived in the forest, and came out only in winter in search of food, and often they had to make big fires all round their hut, to keep them off. He asked her who she was, whence she came, why she was alone, and where she wanted to go. But Corona remained silent, only shaking her head, till the man really imagined she was dumb. At last he asked her if she was hungry, and at that her eyes became so eager, that he smiled kindly. Turning to the smoking pot on the fire, he filled a great wooden bowl with a sort of thick soup, which smelt invitingly, and putting a big wooden spoon into Corona's hand, bade her eat. Corona looked at him gratefully, and gave him such a sweet smile, that the old man cried out:

"There! There! Those eyes say more than words; thou couldst melt the heart of a stone. Eat, now, and I will ask no more questions. My son seems to find thy face fair, certainly, by the way he looks at thee."

The boy started, but Corona smiled down at him so kindly, that, feeling encouraged, he dragged from beneath the bed a store of old but clean rags, and began, not unskilfully, to wrap them round Corona's sore feet, making a rough kind of shoes, like those that Italian peasants wear. Corona longed to say some kind word to him to show her gratitude. The hospitality of the two rough men was infinitely comforting after her dreadful days of loneliness. Then the old man began to talk again, seeming pleased to have some one to listen to him. He told of their simple life, how his wife had died whilst his son Rollo was quite a baby, how he had brought him up as best he could, and how they very seldom saw a living soul. Rollo, who had finished binding Corona's feet, sat on the floor, after having fetched himself a bowl of soup; and joined from time to time in his father's talk. They certainly seemed happy to have a guest.

"There is a legend," continued the old man, "that quite in the middle of the forest there stands a wonderful snow-white temple."

Corona started.

"But," continued the old man, "no one has ever seen it; the forest is so thick, and the animals that live in it are so fierce, that no one has ever had the courage to go far. But they say that the temple has many courts, and that in the middle court lies some hidden treasure, some curious, unknown mystery, and that the person who can reach it will get his heart's desire, and see great things." Corona listened breathlessly, and pressed her hand on her heart. Was she so near the end of her search? Was it really here, here?

"And," the voice of the elder man broke in upon her thoughts, "at first the wood seems beautiful, the trees are so high and straight, and such beautiful birds fly about from branch to branch; but those who try to go too far in never return. That legend of the white temple with its mystery has lured many on to try their luck, but, as I say, none ever return."

The fire crackled with a comfortable sound, the man talked on, and Rollo sat gazing at Corona, whilst the flames threw curious lights and shades on her face, as she eagerly listened to the man's tale. But fearful anxiety grew in her heart as she thought of the dangers that still lay before her. She was already so tired, and her nerves had been so badly shaken by all she had gone through, that she wondered if she might remain a night in the hut to rest, or if the magnet would draw her on again, without leaving her any time to recover. For the moment it lay quite passive in her hand, and in her pocket she felt the little lamp and the piece of yellow glass, both of which in some mysterious way had remained unbroken in spite of all she had endured. By degrees the man's talk grew less animated, and he, too, began gazing into the fire with the natural silence of those who live mostly alone. Corona felt a sort of peace stealing over her whole being, and a great wish to sleep seemed to be pressing down her eye-lids. Rollo noticed this, and told his father that they had better go to work, whilst they let their guest rest in the single bed. Corona accepted readily. Rollo unfastened her cloak, and laid it awkwardly but gently over her, then rolled up some rags to put under her head as a pillow. Never had her golden bed in her father's castle seemed so sweet to Corona as this rough and not over-clean woodman's couch. Hardly had she laid her head down, than sleep took possession of her. Rollo remained, a hand on his hip, gazing upon her fair form, with a growing astonishment in his eyes. His father, roughly, but not unkindly, drew him away.

"Son, son!" he said, "look not too long upon her – she is not for thee! And sometimes, from too much gazing, the eyes later become weary with longing to see that which they can find no more."

Rollo worked hard all that afternoon, but with a curious, restless longing to get back to the hut. He would have liked to ask his father many questions, but a sort of shyness held him back; besides, these two men were unaccustomed to exchange ideas on subjects out of their daily round. Rollo kept wondering why the strange maiden had such fair hair, such a white skin; why her mouth was like a red flower, yet unlike anything he had ever seen. And he remembered the smallness of her feet, as he had washed them, and their velvety softness. He passed his hand over his brow, and stood a moment idle, and all around him seemed alive with a new meaning.

"Rollo," said his father, "work and do not ponder! It is better for thee."

But at sunset they returned to the hut, and it was with eagerness that Rollo opened the low door. There sat the wondrous stranger, on his own little stool, by the glowing embers of the fire. She smiled them a greeting as they entered, regretting bitterly that her vow obliged her

The Steps

to utter silence. She longed to talk to them, to thank them, to express her gratitude; but she could only look at them with her great, sad, brown eyes, which reflected all her emotions. They begged her to stay the night; they would give her their bed, and they themselves would sleep on the floor by the fire. She helped them with the cooking of their simple supper, sorry to be of so little use, as in her royal education with the old philosopher cooking had never even been mentioned. Rollo felt a great longing to beg the beautiful maiden to remain always, never to leave them again, but he dared not express his thoughts – he was unaccustomed to many words. Soon they all went to rest, and once more the young boy had the joy of wrapping Corona up in her cloak on their bed, whilst the father watched half amused, half sad. Then Rollo spread his own rough bearskin over her feet, and laid himself down on the hard floor as near to her as he dared. Corona slept peacefully many hours, but she was awakened by the magnet in her hand, that suddenly seemed full of life and impatience, urging her forwards. She got up hastily, and as noiselessly as she could, realizing that it was best not to wake the sleeping men. But it was with a great pang of regret that she had to leave them thus, and she wondered what she could give them as thanks. She had nothing. And then she thought of her golden, jewelled belt; she slipped it off, and taking a piece of charcoal from the fire, wrote upon the table the words: "God bless you for your kindness!" Laying the belt gently down, she softly crept from the hut, with the weary feeling of the wanderer who must always move on; and regretting that she must seem so base as to run away from those who had been so hospitable to her.

Outside it was still almost dark, but the magnet was very impatient, so that she began to run, only dimly realizing that she was being dragged towards the great forest. Just about sunrise she reached the first trees, and courageously began to pick her way among them, though the woodcutter's words rang in her ears all the time, and she realized the dangers that were awaiting her, wishing she had been able to take Rollo and his father with her. It was, as the man had said, a magnificent forest; she had never seen such wonderful trees, all firs, but so tall, that when she looked up she could hardly see their crowns. Thick moss grew up their trunks, so that all around her seemed bathed in a soft, green light. She noticed, too, that strange plants grew there, unlike those she knew in her own forest at home. Certainly they were larger and more intense in colour, their shapes were strange, different from any she had seen till now. She plucked a beautiful blood-red star, which grew as high as her shoulder; the smell was extraordinarily sweet, but made her feel a little dizzy. Suddenly she saw a golden light flitting from tree to tree, which she discovered was a magnificent bird with large wings and great, soft plumes in its tail; it uttered strange, melodious sounds like a far off call, and other birds answered, flying towards it – birds with dreamlike colours and strange notes. For a time it was such a joy watching them, that Corona, quite unconsciously, walked deep into the forest, and when she turned round she no more saw the point from which she had started. Bushes of beautiful fruit grew close by; Corona wondered if she dared taste them, or if they were poisonous, but being so thirsty, she decided to run the risk; the taste was delicious, and revived her.

The wood grew thicker and thicker, and a great many creeping plants on the ground made her progress difficult, catching her feet and hindering her movements. Nevertheless she would not be discouraged, and till now the beauty of all she saw was ample reward.

Suddenly her foot slipped on something cold and slimy, and she caught hold of a branch to prevent herself from falling. She looked down, and with a gasp of horror found she had trodden on a great snake – a snake of an enormous size and beautiful colour, as everything seemed to be in this wonderful forest. The snake, how ever, did not move – it seemed fast asleep; but a shudder of fear ran all through Corona's body, and she felt afraid of each step she took. Yet what could she do but always press forward? Was not the object of her search near at hand: that wonderful flower which was to bring life back to the loved one and happiness to her sweet sister?

Once more she heard Mora's happy laugh of former days; and remembered also the blanched face of anxiety since Ilario's illness. So, fearful of each step she took, she nevertheless went courageously forward till she came to a beautiful spot, where all the trees were overgrown by great festoons of white roses; and their fallen leaves lay like snow on the ground. They were so large, that Corona could put her whole face within the one she had picked, and they were without thorns. She wished, with a childish longing, that she could show them to her sister; they had both so loved flowers all their lives. All of a sudden a whole cloud of sea-blue butterflies, the size of small birds, began to fly about amongst the white roses; and the sight was so beautiful, that Corona held her breath to watch. They shone as if each one were lit by a light of its own; and their movements, whilst flitting to and fro, were so graceful, that they seemed to be performing some strangely beautiful dance. At last Corona felt quite giddy watching the moving mass of blue and white, so she sank down for a moment on the petal-covered moss. The perfume of the crushed leaves was infinitely delicious, and she buried her hands in the fresh, cool mass of white.

Innumerable turquoise-coloured lizards with bright, gold-rimmed eyes, disturbed by her presence, began running about all around her, much upset by the unexpected intruder. Corona smiled at their evident fright, and began to whistle very softly; then they paused in their flight, and came rapidly towards her, forming a semi-circle around where she sat, and they all seemed to be listening. She felt strangely comforted by their sudden confidence, but dared not move for fear of frightening them away; so she whistled some sweet little melody of her own country. They looked so lovely with their turquoise-coloured bodies glimmering upon the snowy whiteness of the fallen petals, that for a moment Corona forgot all else but the beauty of this fairy-like forest. All around the roses shed their leaves like soft snow-flakes. Suddenly she heard a cracking of branches, and sprang up, easily frightened now by every sound, and the little lizards dispersed in weird, blue patterns; but what she saw advancing towards her only made part of the lovely picture: a snow-white stag, carrying on his head the most prodigious horns imaginable, antlers all of gold. He stood, his head held high, infinitely larger than any stags she had ever heard of, and with great blue eyes, that somehow reminded her of Mora. He really was superb, and looked the proudest thing she had ever seen. She longed to ride on him, and wondered if he would let her approach. She held out the rose she had plucked, and the glorious animal advanced with kingly majesty, and came quite near; but instead of nibbling the rose she offered he passed his rough tongue over her face, and then knelt down before her, as if inviting her to mount. Without hesitation she sprang on to his back with the help of his wonderful antlers; his soft, spotlessly white skin was like velvet to her touch. The moment she was seated the stag rose, and with a swinging stride started off, winding in and out of the trees, cleverly avoiding the branches which threatened to

The Woodcutters

catch his enormous antlers. Corona held on by their help, and she felt strangely confident in this king of the forest who had offered his services to her in so grand and simple a manner. They advanced with great rapidity, Corona wondering if all were well, and if he were taking her where she wished to go. Soon the forest became so thick, the trees grew so close to each other, that they could advance but slowly, and at last the noble creature stopped, being unable to pass any longer, because of the size of his antlers.

Again he bent his knees so that Corona could dismount, which she did with infinite regret, and stroked him lovingly, unable to make up her mind to part from him. He stood like a grand marble statue, his proud head held high, his antlers standing out to the right and left like great rays from the sun. "Beautiful, beautiful beast," thought Corona. "How I wish you could come with me! Then I should no more feel so lonely and afraid!" For a moment he bent his head as if in answer to her unspoken thought, and she kissed him on his forehead where the golden antlers began to grow; his eyes more than ever reminded her of Mora's.

But the magnet was urging her on, so once more she took her lonely road, looking back from time to time to catch a last glimpse of her late companion. He stood immovable, gleaming white between the dark tree trunks, and she said to herself: "Saint Hubert's stag must have stood thus!" And it almost seemed to her as if she saw the cross between his horns. But soon he was hidden by the thickness of the forest, and once more Corona was alone, more lonely even than before, because of those few hours of companionship. The shadows were getting longer, and lay in great black lines across her way, and she realized with anguish that night and its hidden fears were near; and she remembered the kindly hut where she had rested the night before.

But what was that? A creeping sound, something coming towards her – some new terror! Some fresh danger! Yes, there crouching before her she saw a great black leopard, magnificent in its uncanny size, like some enormous cat in a bad dream. With a feeling of faintness Corona leant against a tree, fascinated by those cold, hungry, gleaming, green eyes that stared at her; fascinated by the crouching beast, which seemed ready to spring. Suddenly a companion was at its side, and then another and another; from behind each tree a great black creature appeared to rise out of the ground, watching her with its wicked eyes. Now indeed her last hour must have come; and all her efforts had been in vain, and Ilario would die, and Mora would blind her eyes with weeping. No one would know what had become of her, and her mother would grow old with grief. And Yno! Yes, poor Yno! Faithful little page, what would he feel? The animals crouched as if biding their time, glad to make the horrible uncertainty last. How black they were! And how beautiful their coats! Everything in this forest was so wonderfully beautiful. She pressed her hands against her sides, and as she did so she seemed to feel a strange heat beneath her dress. What was it? She pressed her hand harder; yes, something warm in her pocket; she drew it out – her little lamp! It was the wise woman's lamp, that had suddenly lit of itself. It was a tiny, plain little earthenware lamp, like those found in old Roman graves. Suddenly it shed an extraordinary, strong white light, at the sight of which the huge black creeping creatures drew back with dull roars of discontent. Yes! They were afraid of the white light! Now she understood why the wise woman had given her the lamp. The magnet drew her forward, and in the growing darkness she advanced slowly, holding her little lamp before her; and as she moved the furious leopards retreated, but always keeping her in sight. They were so dark, that their bodies were hardly discernible in the dusk, and looked like shadows creeping beside her. But as the night came on Corona was only aware of their nearness by the glowing light of their eyes; and their tread was so stealthy, that she only heard it when a branch cracked beneath them. But now all the forest seemed alive with the eyes of wild beasts, shining in the dark; they were on all sides, and some came so near, that Corona felt their hot breath on her hands, so that they made the flame of her little lamp flicker, and she was afraid it would be blown out.

By degrees she seemed to get accustomed to this strange company of glowing eyes; only she was becoming terribly weary, and she felt the moment was coming when she would have to give in and rest; and she wondered if the animals would not try, in spite of her lamp, to harm her in some way. There were hundreds of them now, and a curious smell of wild animals seemed to fill the air, and the snapping of dry twigs on the ground became like the crackling of a great fire. It was awful, this silent company of beasts of prey, kept off only by the flickering flame of that small lamp she clutched in her hand. Slower and slower became her tired steps, till at last she stumbled over a fallen tree-trunk, and sank exhausted on the ground. In her fall the lamp seemed for a moment to go out, and immediately she heard a dull roar from hundreds of unseen creatures, and she realized more vividly than ever that the lamp alone stood between her and certain death. But she remained lying where she was, unable to go farther; the little lamp had recovered its steady light. She leaned her head against a tree-stump, and put her lamp beside her, and it shed a small circle of light on the dark ground, but not strong enough to show her any of her unseen, fearful companions. All around her was a circle of glowing eyes – row upon row of them; a muffled sound of breathing filled the night, and their breath reached her from time to time.

She felt as if in a strange and terrible dream; but a curious feeling of unreality helped her to bear the fear that made her poor little heart flutter. The fatigue was such, that, in spite of the terror of her situation, she fell into a deep sleep, her head pillowed against the mossy tree-stump, her white hands folded in her lap, the tiny lamp burning flickeringly at her side. All around the great beasts of prey crouched and watched, wide awake, and their burning eyes were like myriads of fire-flies. Nature was merciful, and she slept peacefully many hours, forgetting her trouble, her fear, and her weariness.

She awoke only as the first streaks of dawn penetrated the cloak of darkness that night had laid over all things, good and bad. She woke with a start, and the sight she saw as her eyes opened was at once fearful and magnificent. In great circles, ten deep, innumerable wild beasts: black panthers and tigers, spotted leopards, and great brown, huge-headed bears, and, more awful than all, round the trunks of trees were wound huge serpents. Corona sat up, and the fearful reality came back to her awakened mind. But her little lamp still burnt bravely on the ground at her side, shedding but little light now that daybreak was at hand.

Again the magnet made itself felt, and forced her to rise and follow its impulse. So she rose, but laid her arm across her face with an instinctive movement of self-defence. But as she advanced with her lamp in her hand, the animals all backed, and although they surrounded her on all sides, and advanced as she moved, none dared to come near enough to touch her. The forest was more beautiful than ever; and the flowers seemed even stranger and larger than those she had seen the day before. The trees, too, had changed, and were such as Corona had never seen; and many seemed breaking beneath a mass of glorious flowers. Corona walked on, always followed by

The Stag

the terrible companions that prowled around her. Shining through the trees she now saw a curious opening, where the mossy ground changed into a greyish red colour, and as she approached she noticed that her troop of followers hung back as if suddenly afraid. But she walked on more hurriedly, and came to a sort of broad road; this she soon realized was strewn with still glowing ashes, and a disagreeable heat beat in her face. It looked like a great bare circle between two parts of the forest, separating one from the other like a sort of barrier, before giving entry to an inner enclosure. But how was she to cross that broad strip of burning cinders? She put one foot forward, but drew it back sharply; the rags that Rollo had wrapped round her feet were already scorched and brown.

Now she understood why her hungry companions had left her; they could not cross this burning ring. But how was she to cross it? Even if her courage did not fail her, she would burn her feet, and then be unable to continue, thus perishing miserably between the fire and wild beasts, and it seemed only a choice between two terrible deaths. She felt sure that if she could only cross this glowing ring she would be near her goal; and it meant life to the loved one, and happiness for her sister and her mother – her sweet, good mother! All her childish need of her mother seemed to sweep over her.

Would she never feel those kind arms round her again? Would she never be able to lay her weary head down on that loving breast, to be comforted and caressed? Would she die here all alone, wild beasts ready to devour her body? She suddenly realized all the infinite desolation of her situation; she felt how small and young and helpless she was; how much to be pitied like a lost child, full of pain and hunger and weariness, and yet not a child, because the pain in her heart was greater than children's grief. She leant against one of the great trees, a tiny speck in that vast forest that stretched behind her, magnificent, dark, and awful, full of terrors and beauty, full of life and death; before her the glowing circle that cut her off from that which she had come to seek.

But she would try again – the soul must be stronger than the body; and she remembered how in olden days maidens were supposed to be able to walk unharmed with bare feet over burning coals. So once more she approached the cruel ring and bravely advanced upon it. An intolerable pain shot through all her body, the rags round her feet blazed up, and she felt that she must perish; that no human strength could bear such suffering. She realized nothing more, except that all was agony, but that advance she must, blindly, as one mad, for whom pain was the only existing reality. Suddenly she felt a curious sensation, as if her body had become so light that her feet no more touched the glowing ashes; and with incredulous eyes she seemed to see the ring retreating beneath her, as if she were soaring over it instead of walking on it. The pain of her scorched feet had been so great, that it numbed all other sensations. She was dreaming, surely! This was the beginning of death. She had often heard that death was merciful; and such it was, because there was no doubt that her feet no more felt the burning cinders, and still the feeling that she was far above the ground continued. No, she was not dying, she was not dreaming. She saw above her head a great moving shadow, and to her unutterable astonishment, and with a new sensation of terror, she realized that she was in the grip of some great bird. She was indeed far above the ground; beneath her she saw the ring of glowing coals, which appeared like an uncanny, coloured ribbon. She was nearly as high as the great trees. But it was no use to struggle – she must resign herself to her fate. She had been through so much lately, that she hardly had the strength left to be afraid. There are certain moments when even fear ceases, because the spirit is too tired to let that cruel sensation master it. Now there was no doubt that she was nearing the ground once more, but softly, without jerks, as if the creature that had her in its clutches were treating her lovingly. The next thing she realized was that she had been gently laid down on a soft, thick bed of emerald green moss, sown with a thousand sweet-smelling, star-shaped little white flowers; and when she looked up, there, soaring above her head, was a great eagle with magnificent wings outstretched, almost immovable, in mid-air. He came lower, so that Corona could see his keen, quiet eyes, that seemed to look at her with tender pity. He hovered around her, circling above her head, quite near; and once he touched the ground, and with his soft, dark wings he tenderly caressed the poor girl's burnt feet, taking away all the pain as if by magic. Then once more he rose, quiet and stately, his great, outstretched wings throwing black shadows on the moss beneath; but he circled higher and higher, till the blue sky seemed to receive him , and Corona saw him no more. Neither did she know that it was the same old, old eagle who had travelled so much, and seen all things beneath the sun – the joy and the pain, the beginnings and the endings. How soft the moss was! How sweet to her tired body! Her feet were now bare, without kind Rollo's roughly made shoes, and they were scorched and black, but the eagle's wings had taken away the pain, and after a little time she felt ready to rise; besides, the magnet that she still held was beginning to urge her on. The little lamp was lying not very far from her; probably it had fallen from her hand when she had been far above ground; it was overturned, and the light had gone out; but it was unbroken because of the thickness of the moss. She picked it up, cooled her feet in a small pool near by, and then started off once more, with an instinctive feeling that her goal was near.

She walked for about an hour, very quickly, because the magnet seemed greatly excited. And now she came to a high wall, so suddenly and unexpectedly, that she was quite startled. The wall was enormously high, and seemed to have no opening, and was grown over with thousands of creeping plants – a beautiful profusion of colours: huge violet and white and light-blue clematis mixed with unnaturally large honeysuckle, that wound itself amongst trailing branches of orange and white roses. Farther on great mauve bunches of wistaria, each about the size of Corona herself, hung down from the top of the wall, like waterfalls of sweet-smelling colour. There were also flowers Corona did not know. She especially admired a wonderful orange-coloured kind, like great, soft, feathery cushions, that grew thickly on long, bramblelike branches without leaves, forming a carpet of colour, in which Corona buried her face, drinking in an exquisitely sweet perfume. And again those glorious, gigantic, snow-white roses, like those she had seen before, amongst the blue butterflies. She lifted one of the great branches, and noticed, to her surprise, that the wall beneath was of beautiful white marble, carved in wonderful, intricate designs – curious, mysterious patterns – the like of which she never remembered having seen before. She walked along the wall, breathing in all the delicious perfumes, often standing still in wonder, absorbing into her soul that feast of colour. She came to a part where, to her delight, hung enormous bunches of purple grapes, one single grape of which was the size of a peach. Their leaves were red and orange and brown, as if painted by some cunning magician who had wished to out-do the sunset's glow. Corona stretched up her arms and detached a few of the grapes, which seemed to concentrate within their flavour the deliciousness of all other fruit. She moved slowly on, seeking for some sort of entrance – some sort of door in this enormous barrier, but found none. Was some mysterious porch hidden beneath this wonderful growth of plants? Would she miss it? She felt anxious, and began lifting the great creepers in a fruitless search. It was very exhausting work, and her arms ached, and again she felt inexpressibly lonely and helpless. But now she came to a corner, which made her realize that the wall was probably built in a square. She pressed on her way bravely, and the masses of fallen petals beside the wall were cool to her naked feet. Often she sank ankle-deep into them, and their different colours lay like a never-ending rainbow before her. Suddenly her anxious gaze discovered far ahead something white and gleaming. She pressed on, new hope filling her once more; but the white object was far off, and it seemed to her impatience that she hardly advanced at all.

Nevertheless, by degrees it took form, and she saw that it was a sort of porch, supported by great white columns, the roof of which was overgrown with masses of creeping plants. Now she began to run in her eagerness. With breathless haste she wound her way between the plants, stumbling over their roots. And now she really reached the porch, the columns of which were of pure white marble, beautifully carved in the same strange designs she had noticed before. And there really was also the very thing she had been seeking – a door! A door in heavy bronze, which had turned a soft green colour, inlaid with patterns of black and white onyx, a wonder of perfect art. It was large and low, beneath an arch of carved marble representing a stiff design of strange birds with outstretched wings, always two and two, their heads turned towards each other, and the space between their wings filled in with beautiful designs in gold. Corona went up to the heavy door, and pressed both hands against it, but it did not yield to her touch; she looked in vain for a handle, a key-hole – none were to be seen. What was she to do? In her despair Corona threw herself

Beats of Prey

down on the ground beneath the porch, folding her hands in her lap with a sigh of infinite discouragement. The marble floor was cold, so cold that she felt it through her clothes. She looked around her, leaving her tired body a moment's rest before concentrating all her efforts again to find ways of opening the door. As she sat there gazing about her, she was attracted by a delicious scent, and saw growing not far from her a strange ruby-red flower, small and round, and as if made of transparent drops of blood. Corona stretched out her hand and picked it carefully, because she felt that if she jerked it roughly the little leaves would fall off and roll away like dew-drops. Certainly the perfume was exquisite, and when she smelt it it seemed as if nothing but the happy visions of her life clustered round her, and as if she heard sweet music in her ears, and as if the pain in the world were less great than the joy. Strange that so many sensations should be held in the perfume of so small a flower. The petals were cool to her touch, and really seemed as if they were round drops of blood. Again Corona bent her head to drink in the fragrance, and she shut her eyes, and lost herself for a moment in sweet recollections, that brought a faint smile to her sad lips. The secret of the little flower was that its perfume was made up out of all the sweet scents that had ever crossed her life. Then bravely she got up, ready to try her fortune once more, and approached the merciless door, holding the tiny red flower in her hand.

As she came near, the door seemed suddenly to tremble, and Corona, quite unintentionally, touched it with the flower. No sooner had the red petals come in contact with it than it flew open noiselessly and as if by magic. A vision of infinite beauty met Corona's eyes; a snow-white temple, separated from her by a deep moat of dark-green water, over which a marble bridge led straight from the bronze door. All round the temple, growing against its snowy walls, was a line of fire-coloured lilies, that stood like great sentinels guarding some hidden treasure. And opposite to the door she had just opened, on the other side of the moat, stood another door, very much of the same workmanship as the first. Corona felt quite weak with emotion at being suddenly near the end of her weary quest, so that some minutes passed before she was able to move; and she drank in all the beauty around her. The temple was of an architecture strange to her, richly carved in beautiful designs. With trembling steps she crossed the bridge, gazing into the clear green water, which reflected the vision of her own sweet face. She hardly recognized it, because of her short hair. It seemed to her an almost unknown face gazing at her; the eyes were unnaturally large and expressive, like all eyes that have gazed upon terrifying sights; like all eyes that have faced in the dark their own tortured souls.

She reached the opposite door that stood grim and stern confronting her; it was also a work of art, inlaid with gold, and on each side the fire-coloured lilies, that were as tall as herself, stood like dumb guardians of a magic world. Again Corona touched the door with her sweet-smelling flower, and it, too, flew open, revealing a marvellous courtyard surrounding another building of the same kind as the first, also snow-white, only more rich than the one she had just entered – more dazzlingly white. Here also ran a moat all round the square court; and the pavement she stood on and the sides of the moat were all of black marble; and over all, bursting out between the slabs of marble, hanging down into the water, tumbling in profusion over the narrow bridge, trailing their long branches everywhere, were roses, roses – blood-red, redder than anything Corona had ever seen; so red that their reflection on the black marble seemed like little pools of blood; they were so red that they looked almost cruel in their extravagant beauty. Corona noticed, with a thrill of fear, that the next door was guarded by two great black panthers, like her terrible companions of the night before, and the door they guarded was of some dull-black metal, marvellously wrought in gold; and over it hung great heavy masses of the same crimson roses, swinging their great creepers against its dark surface, dropping their petals, like drops of blood, on the dark fur of the magnificent, velvety panthers. The doorstep also was one brilliant mass of roses, that grew in wild profusion. Corona, remembering her lamp, drew it from her pocket, and immediately it lit with the strange white light. So, fearlessly she approached the growling monsters, in one hand her lamp, in the other her precious red flower. Corona touched the door, and it, too, flew silently open, whilst the black panthers crouched down as if afraid. This time she stood in a court of exquisite green onyx, so smooth and bright and polished, that she seemed to be standing on water; all around her, creeping over the walls, and trailing their great bunches on the ground, were branches of light blue, sweet-smelling wistaria. When she had gazed down into the moat, she saw it was full of blue water-lilies, whose great stars stood wide open, revealing their treasure of golden stamens; and they reposed on their great, cool, green leaves, that had the same delicate tints as the onyx.

The door on the other side of the moat was of beaten silver, encrusted with large, curiously entwined circles of moon stones; and at each side, jealously guarding the entrance, stood a kingly tiger in magnificent ferocity. The skins of the two splendid beasts had orange and golden tints, like autumn leaves, and the black stripes looked like thin snakes. When they moved, strange lights seemed to play upon them, as if the snakes were alive. Corona felt as if she were in a dream, and all her fear seemed to have gone from her, but she was very pale, and her beautiful eyes had dark circles of suffering beneath them. She held her little lamp before her, mounted the step that led to the door, and touched it lightly with her magic flower. It flew open as the others had done – noiselessly, easily, and Corona stood spellbound. This court was all of pink marble, so delicate in tint, that it reminded one of the glow on the cheek of a babe just aroused from its sleep. From between the marble slabs grew beautiful spreading trees covered with pink and white blossom; and the trees were bound together with delicate, pink, creeping roses. Over hanging the moat they tumbled in sweet, rambling masses to the calm water, where they mingled with the pink water-lilies that grew beneath them; and they seemed like sisters greeting each other, each enjoying the other's beauty.

All along the nearer wall stood rows of peony plants, breaking beneath the weight of their delicately tinted pink blossoms; and thousands of black butterflies, swarming around them, were the only dark touches in the whole place. Corona longed to linger; it seemed a place to rest in and be happy – a place made by the angels, and where all thoughts must be pure. There were soft sounds of falling leaves all about, and the dark butterflies circled and circled around, casting small shadows upon the pink marble flags. But the magnet urged her forward, and Corona hurried over the bridge to the next door, which was of pink mother-of pearl, apparently made out of a single piece; and a beautiful design of roses and thorns was inlaid upon it, in ivory and gold. Guarding it stood two big grey bears, with enormous heads and small watchful eyes. But Corona was now quite fearless, and holding her lamp so that its white light protected her she touched this door also, which flew open. It was the fourth court

The Door

she now entered, and its aspect was that of an exquisitely beautiful graveyard. It was all of white marble, which had taken the delicate tints of wax and old ivory. Among the marble flags tall, dark, black-green cypresses grew like great fingers pointing towards the sky; and between them were a great number of curious grave-stones, like altars; they were of various sizes and heights, but all had the same long, rectangular shape. Upon each stood a great white jade bowl, in which burnt some mysterious incense that exhaled a delicious odour, mounting in transparent, blue clouds of smoke towards the sky. Round each grave white roses clustered and climbed, covering most of the strange inscriptions that were carved on the top of the slabs. All around smoked the beautiful bowls, sending their little, faintly coloured columns of smoke soaring upwards, so that each monument looked like an altar dedicated to some unknown god. Corona felt an indescribable sadness pass over her soul, and she longed to press her living lips upon each grave of these unknown dead as she passed, so that they should receive the offering of her pity.

"But," then, she sadly said to herself, "perhaps they are happier than I!" And she stretched her arms towards Heaven with a gesture of mute prayer. Everything there seemed to be mounting towards that blue sky of promise: the dark cypresses, the blue smoke in the precious bowls, Corona's outstretched arms, and the mute cry of supplication that came from her soul. But she dared not tarry; she only moved for a moment amongst the tombs, caressing them with hands that touched them tenderly, as if instinctively remembering that each contained a heart that had once beat with human love; and in remembrance also of the tears that had no doubt been shed upon each.

Then she crossed the bridge over the moat, and came to a door of pure white ivory encrusted with golden birds, like those she had noticed on the arch when she entered. There, stern guardians of the entry, majestic and immovable, sat two snow-white lions, still and grand, with such calm faces, that Corona felt a great wish to caress them, as if they were dogs. Instead she touched the beautiful door, which also obeyed the small ruby-red flower, and opened wide to reveal the fifth court. For a moment Corona dared not enter, so dazzled was she. The walls, the floor, the sides of the moat were all of glorious beaten gold; and the flowers that grew there were violet and mauve and purple. There were rows of violet asters in bushes taller than Corona; then long lines of exquisite irises, all growing straight, and proud of their own marvellous colouring, each keeping jealously away from the other, so that its beautiful shape should stand out undisturbed by its neighbour. Over the walls hung clematis in dark, velvety richness, trailing its creepers in glorious masses into the water, where the leaves floated like small boats, reminding Corona with a pang of longing of the colour of the sail of her own boat, on which was woven the golden, cross-shaped sword, the emblem of her proud family. But now a trembling seized her, because she knew that the next door led to the Lily of Life. The next door meant the end of her quest; meant the fulfilment of her wish; meant the last struggle; meant either success or defeat, life or death. Behind that last door was all her hope and all her fear. Behind that closed door the mystery would be revealed! All her strength seemed to leave her, and for a while she stood, too weak to move, her heart beating like a great, cruel hammer within her. She tried to walk, but her knees gave way beneath her, and she sank down on the bridge, her head pressed against the arch over it; and the dark purple clematis seemed to nestle round her head, pitying and loving her, touching her softly with its beautiful petals, sending out delicate tendrils to caress her white neck, which the short hair no longer protected. The magnet had fallen from her hands, useless now that she was before that door, and lay like a dead piece of metal at her feet; but the sun touched it for a moment, drawing small sparks of light from it, which shone like diamonds. The little lamp had gone out, its work also done. Before that last door, which was of gold, worked like a great sun, all the rays converging towards the centre, where a great, many-hued opal seemed to guard some hidden fire, stood two spotless angels, their white robes falling in straight folds to the ground, two great wings spread high over their heads, and two others hiding their feet. When Corona lifted her head, she met eyes full of infinite pity and love. Fascinated by their quiet majesty, she rose to her feet, and slowly, hesitatingly, she advanced towards them, her gaze riveted upon their shining figures, her great, sad eyes asking all the questions that her tongue might not form into words. Between her fingers she still held the little, red, sweet-smelling flower, which she felt was useless now. As she neared the door, the two angels gently touched it with their hands in the centre, where the opal seemed to hide its fire, and as their ivory-white hands were laid upon it it opened.

Slowly, slowly it gave way – Corona's heart beat, beat – and she stood at last within the inner court. Here all seemed bathed in a strange moonlight, a sort of blue glare came from the middle of a dark, square pool; but each time Corona tried to look at the centre of the pool an intolerable pain shot through her eyes and brain, so that she turned her back upon it to be able first to realize her surroundings. How strange it was! She seemed to have left all the sunshine outside, and here it was suddenly night; certainly not a dark night, but a night lit up by the blue-white light of the moon. The enclosure she had entered was like some exquisite cloister. Snow-white arches, supported upon marble columns, ran all the way round, and each column and each arch was carved with a different design. It had the appearance of a curious temple, yet the shape was like that of the cloisters of a monastery, and the whole was flagged with marble, as white and shining as a freshly fallen sheet of snow. All the columns, in their straight rows, gleamed like immovable ghosts in the pale light. An oppressive stillness hung over all, and the whole place seemed filled with a strangely sweet perfume, so strong that it made Corona's brain reel. At the foot of each column, and as immovable, stood a spotless, white peacock with a great, fan-like tail, spread out in all its majesty.

Once more Corona turned towards the dark, square pool, the water of which was on a level with the marble pavement. But this time she held up the yellow glass to her eyes, and then she gazed – gazed.

In the middle of the black water, growing in stately solitude, was a lily – a lily from which an intensely brilliant light seemed to pour. A lily so dazzling, so perfect, so supernaturally pure, that the only sensation that possessed the soul at the sight was the desire to sink on one's knees and adore it. It was larger than any lily Corona had ever seen, but of the same shape and kind as those she had in her own garden at home. Yet before this one her heart seemed to feel an extraordinary peace, an extraordinary longing for better things, a wonderful happiness that spread through body and soul, giving her the sensation that she was a spirit from a better world, with no desire but to let her heart melt in infinite gladness in a song of praise. She knelt down at the water's edge, hid her face in her hands, and cried, cried tears that seemed to wash away all the evil in human nature,

The Tombs

all the suffering and pain, all the struggles, all the partings and disappointments. And all her own grief seemed to melt away, relieving her overburdened heart of its suffering. And as her tears touched the marble floor, they turned into pure pearls – pearls like those the wise woman wore round her neck; they rolled one by one into the black water, each forming little circles of light on the dark surface; and the circles spread, widened, rippling away in silver, dwarf-like waves.

But soon she dried her tears, for she knew that to get to the flower she must descend into those dark depths, and once more the horror of death seemed to cross her soul. There was no magnet to urge her on – it lay heavy and quiet in her pocket; her will alone could now sustain her. So she quietly unfastened her cloak and laid it down on the marble floor, and stood in her golden under-dress, all torn and stained and soiled by her terrible wanderings. Then, shutting her eyes, so as not to be blinded by the Lily, she sprang bravely into the pool, and sank deep in the water.

It was an awful moment, full of silent horror, worse than anything she had felt since the beginning of her journey, and at each moment she expected to sink, a pale corpse, to the bottom of that deep, watery grave. But just as she was giving up all hope she felt one foot touch a step, and with an effort she moved forward to the next step, so that her head kept above water; and – yes! – now she could advance; she had her feet on a stair leading to the centre. With her eyes tightly shut she moved forward, blindly keeping her direction by the exquisite perfume of the flower. Step by step she advanced. Step by step – slowly, slowly. Now the glare that came from the flower was so awful that it burned through the girl's eye-lids, seeming to pierce her head in two places, as if with sharp daggers. But she was near now! She reached out her arm, and her fingers, seeking their way in the water, found – oh, marvellous moment of attainment! – the stem of the Lily of Life. It yielded beneath her touch, snapping in two as if made of glass. . . .

What happened then Corona never knew. All the air seemed full of strange and beautiful music, and a radiant light seemed to spread over all things. Corona knew not if she were sinking or rising, her body had no weight; the water was no longer cold. All around there seemed to be white wings and sweet voices like the voice of her little brown bird, but a whole chorus of them, as if the heavens were open. The next thing Corona realized was that she was lying couched upon the wings of great, snow-white swans; and that in her hand she held the Lily of Life, which now her eyes could look upon. Before her in the midst of the pool stood, straight and gleaming, another lily, which had sprung up in the place of the one she had plucked, ready for the next wanderer who had the courage to seek it; ready for the next weary heart that should come, sustained by his belief in its power to comfort.

Sunlight now shone radiantly golden around, so that the marble columns and arches, the slabs on the ground, the water in the pool, were lit up with a bright, yellow light, transforming the ghostly temple into a place of wondrous sweetness. Corona lay still on her bed of white wings and gazed on all the beauty. Her eyes could face the new lily now that her hands clasped the one she had come to seek. She lifted it to her face, and when it touched her infinite gladness seemed to fill her soul, and her wondering eyes discovered that her soiled dress had changed into a robe of spotless whiteness, so soft and pure and bright, as if woven out of the rays of the moon. And more wonderful still, her beautiful golden hair had grown again, thick and full of sunshine, as in the happy days of her childhood, and it rippled over her, as if in a luxuriant cloak of pure, shining metal. And all the time the air seemed full of marvellous music and voices, mingling in a song of praise, but ethereal and almost unreal. Now she was being lifted up by the swans, fearlessly lying on their great wings, and borne away over the beautiful temple. And as they flew she looked down upon all the courts that she had passed, and each stood out clearly in its different colour, but they appeared quite small, like miniature playthings. And now it was the great forest she was being carried across – a great stretch of dark green, hiding all its beauties and all its fears. And now, suddenly, she saw far beneath her the wood-cutter's tiny hut, and a great wish came to her to stay a moment and, her tongue being once more loosened, to offer her thanks to the two kind men who had given her their rough hospitality. She begged the swans to set her down a moment beside the lowly dwelling. They obediently did as she desired, and once more Corona stood before the low door and knocked, and once more it was opened by Rollo, who started back as if in fear. Corona stretched out her hand.

"It is I," she said, "the weary guest thou didst tend so kindly. Let me enter; I would thank thee and thy kind father. I stood beneath a spell, having made a vow of silence, and like a thief I had to steal from your hut, in the dark, whilst you slept. But now my quest is over, and I return to my father's palace." And she told them her name. But they were so overcome by her radiance, as she stood there in her snowy robe and her wealth of golden hair, the Lily in her hand, that, believing her one of God's angels, they fell on their knees before her and kissed the hem of her dress. Then the swans bore her away far up into the blue sky, so that the two men had to shade their eyes to follow the dizzy flight. Father and son stood long, gazing at the spot where she had disappeared; then the old man turned to Rollo and said:

"God has loved us, my son, because he allowed one of his pure angels to enter our hut."

And then they both silently took their axes and went about their work, still awed and wondering.

On flew the swans over the dreadful, frozen sea; over that land of cold and ice; over the wood where Corona had rested; over the desolate, burning plain where she had walked, stumbling against the rolling stones. At last the sea came in sight; and on the forsaken-looking shore stood Yno! – Yno, who in his despair had not moved all this time from the spot where his loved mistress had disappeared, meaning to die there if she had gone for ever. And now he heard the sound of wings, and like a small, white cloud slowly approaching the great, wild swans came in sight, bearing something between them upon a dark blue cloak. Gently they descended, always nearer and nearer to where he stood, and when he saw what it was that they were carrying it seemed to him as if his heart would break with a joy too great to bear. At last the swans tenderly laid down the dark-blue cloak, and there stood Corona, his mistress, his sweet mistress! but with something about her which awed him to silence. Her face seemed radiant with light from another world, and the long white dress seemed too pure to touch, and her great, brown eyes shone out of her pale face with a sadness that he hardly dared meet; and in her hand she held a lily that seemed made of light. But her sweet smile was the same, and she came towards him with the voice he had always known:

"Yno, dear Yno! Thou hast waited for me, and, see, I have come back, and I bring with me that which will give life to one dear to me, and happiness to another also inexpressibly dear to me. God has been merciful and led me through many dangers and many fears, so

The Return

that I have reached what I was seeking; and the terror I have gone through, and all the pain I have borne, and all the silence and solitude, lie behind me as in a dream; and this white robe that came to me I know not how seems a sign of God's mercy. Yno, dear, faithful heart! Now thou must follow me on my last journey towards those that await me. I see the wise woman's boat is there ready to take us home. Come, let us enter it."

Yno clung to her knees, now no longer afraid of her spirit-like appearance; and all his joy, and all his past anxiety and terror for her, he expressed in wild, almost incoherent words, as he pressed his face to the folds of her white robe. And gently, gently, she caressed his bent head, murmuring sweet words of consolation, whilst her gaze wandered across the stretch of ink-blue sea, with a look of yearning and apprehension, which cast a shadow upon her radiance. Then, turning to the wild swans, she thanked them for their help, kissing each one upon its snowy head, and they stretched their long necks up to her as if they would have liked to speak. Now the boat bore the beautiful maiden away over the calm sea, and the wild swans rose in the air, the rays of the sun gilding their outstretched wings, till they were but tiny specks lost in the sky. Corona held Yno's hand between hers, and related to him all she had seen and done – all her fears and fatigues; but especially all the beauty her eyes had beheld, touching but lightly upon all her sufferings.

And the little waves kissed the sides of the boat as it glided forward with great speed, as if anxious to bring the beautiful girl back to her home. Corona's eyes were fixed upon the horizon with an eager, anxious look, but Yno could not keep his gaze from her face, which seemed strangely changed, with suffering written upon it, although none of its beautiful youth was gone. But she seemed to him less human than when she had left him, as if the soul were consuming the body. Her white hands, in which his brown one lay, also seemed to tell a tale of suffering, and from time to time he reverently pressed his lips upon them. And still the boat moved onwards, bringing them nearer to their destination.

After many hours, about sunset, when the sky was taking beautiful, rosy tints, they saw rising before them, shining in golden beauty, the King's castle. Corona uttered a little cry of joy; it seemed to her as if she had been gone for years, and yet not many days had passed since she rushed blindly down those golden steps – that sad, sad night when she tore herself away from all she loved, to begin her pilgrimage of love and silence.

The boat was nearing the shore; the green marble terraces were distinctly visible; Jacob's ladder shone in the last rays of the sun, between its line of dark cypresses. Now the boat touched the sand, and Yno lifted Corona out. A thousand conflicting feelings had taken possession of her – joy and hope and happiness – and she pressed her hand upon her heart to control its furious beating. Was she in time? Was Ilario still alive? Had he perhaps recovered? And had all her sacrifice been useless? And the only words that came from her lips were, "Mother, mother!" It was the great cry of all her nature, of all her anxious soul; it contained all her hopes and all her fears. And then, holding the Lily of Life in her hand, she began running up the golden steps – up, up, as if she had wings. She rushed up the green terraces, and once more, from the bottom of her longing soul, she cried, "Mother!" The window of the Queen's room burst open; that cry had pierced the walls; that cry was the echo of the mother's anxious heart. And a few minutes later Corona lay in those dear arms she had so longed for. She lay there like a quite small child, and it seemed to her as if never again could any harm come to her.

"Mother, does he live?" was her anxious question, as she raised her tear-stained face.

"Yes, my child; but each day he becomes weaker. Now he lies quite still as one already dead, with his eyes closed, and does not even seem to hear Mora's voice; and Mora is wasting away because of her double grief – Ilario's illness and thy absence. My sweet Corona. My child, my child, God be praised that thou hast come back!"

And the Queen raised the beautiful face with both her hands, and gazed long into it, and she, too, realized the change Yno had seen, and a feeling of awe and fear gripped her soul. This beauty seemed of another world; this beauty was almost unbearably pure to the mother's heart. And then Corona told her mother that she had brought the Lily of Life, and begged to be taken to the sick man's room. As they mounted the stairs. Corona clutched her mother's hand, but said not a word, nor did her mother press her with questions; and as they neared the room her steps seemed to hesitate, and her mother looked anxiously into her pale face. But her answer was a sweet smile, and she laid her hand upon the door-handle, and then turning said: "Mother, I pray thee let me go in alone." And the Queen did as she wished, and silently descended the stairs. The news of Corona's return had already aroused a feverish excitement and joy all over the castle.

As Corona entered the sick room. Mora rose to her feet with a cry of joy, and fell sobbing into her sister's arms. But on the bed lay Ilario, like a beautiful marble figure, his splendid features rigid and pale, his long, slim body wasted away, his hands inert and still, his copper-brown locks spread over the white pillow, like dark sea-weed, and his long lashes made great dark lines beneath his eyes. Oh, how beautiful he was! How beautiful, beautiful! Corona felt all her great love mount like a wave within her, overcoming every other feeling. She felt as if she must fall down and kiss that marble face; that she must lay her head upon that still heart; and then for one horrible moment she thought he was already dead.

"No, no," whispered Mora, clinging to her and understanding her thought; "he still lives, but the flame of life within him flickers, as if at any moment the smallest breath would blow it out! Corona, Corona, hast thou, then, found that which will bring him back to me?"

And as she pronounced that word "me" Corona felt a dagger pierce her heart. Now she bent down over the still form, and gently, with the Lily of Life, touched his brow, his eyes, his lips, his heart, his hands, and hardly had she done so when a marvellous change came over the prostrate figure, the face took its usual colour, the rigid limbs relaxed, and suddenly he sat up, and then sprang to his feet, standing tall and slender and vigorous once more in his crimson gown. And with a cry of joy, "Mora!" he had thrown his arms round his bride, and her head was upon his breast, and his warm, living kisses covered her hair, her face, her lips. . . .

Corona stood by the window, and the last rays of the sun threw a halo round her head, but her eyes had a far-off look, and were turned towards the sea, and the petals of the Lily of Life fell one by one to the ground, and lay like flakes of snow at her feet.

Soon the whole castle was in a great uproar of delight, and all the rooms, so silent since Ilario's illness, rang once more with gay voices, and laughter was heard echoing along the passages and halls. Servants ran backwards and forwards, and pompous courtiers fussed about, asking useless questions and giving useless orders.

Great trumpets were sounded from the towers, proclaiming Ilario's recovery and announcing the marriage for the next day. The King was happy, for they had had sad times, and he cared for the sound of laughter, and although his heart was good and kind he did not like the silence that grief brings in its train. He sat in the great hall, giving orders for the ceremony of the next day, and his eyes feasting on the sight of his two beautiful daughters, and he felt rich and blessed. But the Queen, who saw deeper, with a woman's understanding and a woman's instinct, moved about as one afraid of entering the sanctuary of grief. Corona behaved as though she had never been away; as if no sacrifice had been asked of her. And when she was pressed with questions relating to her wanderings, she spoke of the beautiful flowers she had seen; of the white stag that had carried her on his back; of the little brown bird whose voice was like the song of angels; of the wood-cutters' kindness; and the soft moss that had been restful to her feet. But the pain she had borne, and the fear and the anguish, she kept hidden in her heart, so that no shadow should fall on this day of rejoicing.

And that night, after the dancing was over, she went to their own room with Mora, and long the two sisters sat together and recalled all their love for each other, and Mora wept at the thought of the parting so near at hand. But Corona spoke of the joy awaiting her in her new country, and in words that came with difficulty reminded her sister of Ilario's love. And that night she herself tucked Mora into the little golden bed in which she was sleeping for the last time, and long she sat beside it, till Mora fell asleep, and then Corona bent down to kiss the tears that were wet on her sister's cheeks. And all the time it seemed to her as if some cruel hand were in her breast, pressing her heart in an iron grip, till she could hardly breathe. Very softly

The Recovery

she now went to her mother's room, and found her kneeling beside her bed; a small, shaded lamp lit up the beautiful chamber with a mysterious light. Long the two women gazed into each other's eyes, and they stood at the open window together, looking at the stars in the sky, and both knew that words were impossible, and that silence alone could express what they had to say to each other. At last, softly, the mother said:

"My child, thou must go to rest. To-morrow thou needest all thy strength." And she kissed her with all her love, and gently made the sign of the cross upon her brow.

The next day awoke with a glorious sunrise, and the whole sky was red and orange; tiny grey clouds flitted across the face of the sun, the sea blazed, and the flowers sent up their sweetest perfume and spread out their most brilliant colours.

In the room where all their youth had been spent together Corona decked her sister with her own hands, and the radiant Mora stood in the sunlight, her beautiful white dress flowing around her, and upon her shoulders Corona fixed a silver mantle worked with pearls, and upon her head she placed a soft, white veil, that covered the jet-black hair, and a crown of diamonds, that sparkled with a thousand lights, and flashed so that one could hardly look at it. And then the handmaidens put a white robe on Corona also, but on the breast of hers was embroidered in gold an eagle, that held between its claws a bleeding heart – the design she had formerly worked herself in the days that were no more. Upon her head they laid a crown of lilies, but no veil covered the golden mantle of hair, that hung down far below her waist.

The door opened, and Ilario came to claim his bride – Ilario as they had seen him the first day, clad in his golden armour; the sun flashed upon the metal, and he looked like St. George come down to earth once more. Corona shut her eyes, as if the brightness were too much for her to bear. But Ilario came towards her, and, as at the meeting in the forest, bared his head and bent his knee before her, and thanked her for the life she had restored to him. And again Corona smiled, and answered:

"May my blessing go with what I love most dearly in all the world." But Yno, who stood in the doorway, felt as if he would cry aloud in pain.

In a beautiful pageant of many colours the wedding procession wound itself towards the church. The Princesses rode on their favourite steeds, and when Jorio saw his mistress once more he neighed with joy, and she patted his glistening neck, and for the first time tears gathered in her eyes.

When all was over, they came back to the castle, and a great banquet was given in the stone hall, where the old flags hung from the ceiling; and Ilario had his bride on his right, and on his left sat Corona, but she did not touch the food set before her. Sweet music filled the room, and on the table a carpet of dark-red roses almost hid the golden cloth. Corona's hand played amongst them, and when the dark petals fell between her white fingers they seemed to her like drops of blood coming from her own heart, and she remembered also how they had lain in brilliant spots upon the black panthers which guarded one of the doors of the temple, and a great longing came to her to hear the little brown bird's voice, that had always seemed to ease her pain. Behind her chair stood Yno, and sadly he changed the golden plates upon which her food remained untouched. But each time that the Queen, who was sitting opposite, searched her gaze, it was to receive a sweet, brave smile in response. Only when the preparations were being made for the ball, which was to end that day of re-joicings, did Corona slip out of the castle and go to Jorio's stable, and there, her face hidden in his golden mane, the colour of her own hair, she gave vent at last to her tears. Animals need no words of explanation; that was why Corona had sought refuge with her horse. Long she remained there, her arms round the horse's neck, her face buried close against his warm body; and the smell of his skin reminded her of all the days of her happiness.

The ball was magnificent. Every one came from far and wide, and brilliant colours filled the room, and the music seemed untiring, like the feet of those who danced. And the bride stood beside the golden-clad knight, and received a hundred congratulations; but all the time she would have Corona's hand in hers. Then came the moment when the newly married couple were to be led down to the seashore, where a boat awaited them, ready to bear them over the sea to the country which was now to be Mora's home. Between the tall cypresses that bordered the golden staircase flamed torches, and the steps were strewn with sweet-smelling lavender and jasmine, and garlands of roses were hung from tree to tree. And music played, and beautiful voices sang from out of the dark, mingling with the sound of the distant sea. The two sisters walked down hand in hand; Ilario had gone before to receive his bride on the boat; and Mora begged her sister to come soon to visit them in her new home. With each step it seemed to Corona that she was bidding farewell to part of her life. On the seashore stood the King and Queen and all the court. The beautiful boat was draped with sumptuous hangings, and flowers had been strewn everywhere. At the helm of the boat was the figure of an angel with wings stretched backwards, and in the angel's hands was a cross of light, that was reflected in broken lines upon the dark sea. From the boat also sounded sweet music; and a soft wind raised the silken draperies, and made the colours shine where the light of the lanterns fell upon them.

For the last time the sisters stood side by side on that shore, which had known them as laughing children. Ilario came forward and took leave of the King and Queen and their courtiers, who then slowly mounted the golden steps, so as to wave a last farewell to the boat from the brilliantly lit terrace above. Only Corona still stood holding her sister's hand; but she knew that all was over, that nothing could help her now that she must part from all that life meant to her. Ilario came to her, and a sudden anguish of comprehension crossed his face, but he met her brave eyes, and then he bent his head and pressed his parting kiss upon her lips. As he did so, it seemed to Corona as if her heart were beating its last, and yet it was the sweetest moment of her life. . . .

The boat moved from the shore, its lights and brilliant colours were reflected in the dark water, and seagulls flew all around it, their white wings flashing when they came into the circle of light.

Corona stood alone, that kiss burning on her lips. The boat had been swallowed up into the darkness of the night, the wind played amongst her hair, and the sea-birds' voices seemed the last strains of music reaching her from the boat which carried away her happiness. She heard not her mother calling to her from above – calling, calling, with a voice full of love and fear. On receiving no answer, the Queen, being a woman, and knowing that certain griefs are best borne alone, sadly followed the King into the castle, where now all was still, and where the smell of faded flowers alone filled the air.

The night was dark, and Yno groped his way down the golden stairs, where the torches had burnt out and the garlands of roses

Corona

were letting their petals fall softly one by one. He reached the seashore, and there – oh, God! – lay the sweet form of his mistress, and the first rays of the rising moon shone upon her face. It was deathly white, but her pale lips were parted as if with a smile of happiness, and both her beautiful hands were clasped upon her heart – her broken heart.

In the morning a great search was made for Corona. Two bodies were found on the silver sand – Yno with his faithful head upon the small feet he had followed so often; and upon the breast of the beautiful maiden sat a tiny brown bird, and sang, sang – with a voice that told the mother's breaking heart that her daughter had found treasures beyond their reach. . . .

On a lonely shore far off stood the wise woman, her black veil hanging like a dark shadow behind her tall form, and as the sun rose in the sky she seemed to see a wonderful column of snow-white wings mounting towards Heaven; and through the air, down towards where she stood like a lonely figure of grief, came music so sweet, so exquisitely perfect, that it was like a hymn of hope to her frozen heart; like a great song of forgiveness sent from above. And the air all around seemed to echo the one word, "Corona, Corona," and the sea caught it up: "Corona, Corona," and the wind answered, "Corona." And the seagulls, seeing the great column of white wings, flew upwards, trying to reach it, but in vain, because it was at the doors of Heaven.

Then the wise woman returned slowly to her boat, to await the day when her soul also would be borne upwards, washed of its sin – redeemed by the help she had brought unto others. . . .

CPSIA information can be obtained
at www.ICGtesting.com
Printed in the USA
LVHW051508171218
600755LV00026B/967/P